MW01132430

small town
KilleR
Jim Keane

2024, TWB Press

www.twbpress.com

Small Town Killer
Copyright © 2024 by Jim Keane

All rights reserved. No part of this story may be reproduced or transmitted in any form or by any means, electronic or mechanical, including photocopying, recording, or by any information storage and retrieval system, without written permission of the author, except in the case of brief quotations embodied in critical articles or book reviews.

This is a work of fiction. Names, characters, places, and incidences are either a product of the author's imagination or are used fictitiously. Any resemblance to any actual person, living or dead, events, or locales is entirely coincidental.

Edited by Terry Wright

Cover Art by Terry Wright
Background image from shutterstock.com

ISBN: 978-1-959768-32-6

Chapter One

S canning the newspaper while waiting for the bank to open, Jesse Curley sat in his beat-up '82 Corolla parked at Peekskill's Apple Farm Commons off Highway 9. It wasn't the latest headlines on high gas prices or an economy teetering on a recession that interested him. Instead, one article had him deeply engrossed.

BRAZEN BRONX ROBBERY NETS $200,000 IN THROUGH-THE-ROOF HEIST. Woodlawn, Bronx. Police seek individuals who robbed a bank by cutting a hole in the roof. "They cut through the metal and concrete vault then stole several safety deposit boxes and cash," said Chief Bernard Kelly, NYPD Detectives Bureau.

The words created images that leaped off the page and into his brain. The audacity of these crooks who dared and risked everything, the sheer nerve, cutting through the bank roof and escaping with the cash, ignited a thrill in him. *What a payday. What balls. What a rush.* His heart pounded with a mix of intrigue and admiration.

He glanced beyond the mundane façades of

Hudson River Bagels, Chinatown Kitchen, and the flower shop to the Peekskill Bank, where a Brinks truck rumbled at the curb. Armed with handguns, two jacked men wearing Kevlar vests loaded money bags onto a cart.

His pulse quickened. He dropped the paper onto an old blanket in the back seat, rubbed his sweaty hands on his jeans, and snatched up his last unemployment check. Unwanted memories flooded his mind:

Six months ago, he'd encountered his co-worker trudging out of the boss's office with his head down. "What's wrong, Ryan?"

He ran a hand across his sweaty face. "It's a bloodbath in there."

Jesse's stomach churned as he readied himself to enter the office of Walter Rickman, Network Manager for Vericom. Rickman never called anyone into his office unless he needed a favor or something was wrong. Rumor had it, with this shitty economy, they'd be laying off half the staff. *Oh, God, please, no.* He was already in debt up to his ears.

Once inside the cramped room, he sat hunched forward and regarded Rickman, a lean man with thick glasses, sitting behind an ornate desk, fingers interlaced on his chest. Patches of black hair sprouted from his balding crown. "Mr. Curley, good of you to be on time."

"What's going on?"

"The Network Department is cutting operational costs." Rickman sat back on his throne and folded his arms. "As a result, we're eliminating several positions at this data center. Unfortunately, your job is on the chopping block."

Jesse clenched his fists. "You're running a skeleton crew as is. I've been doing the work of three people. Is this the thanks I get?"

"You're a good worker. Always available when I need extra help, but Corporate says you've got to go. I tried cutting expenses elsewhere, but..." He shrugged.

"But you didn't try hard enough." Jesse had said it like he was spitting out sour grapes.

"Hey. I'm not happy about all these layoffs either."

Jesse scowled. "You're not getting away with this. The union won't stand for it." He stood. "Just wait 'til I contact my shop steward. Shit's gonna hit the fan."

"Sit down, Curley."

"I'll see you in court."

"Don't be a fool. Our lawyers will eat you alive."

Jesse leaned on the desk and went nose-to-nose

with his soon-to-be ex-boss. "We have a contract that assures us job security, especially those of us with seniority."

Rickman scoffed. "There's a clause in the contract that states Vericom can do what it deems necessary for the sake of its stockholders. Besides, your seniority isn't worth squat."

Jesse's throat tightened. "For five years...I've busted my ass for this company, worked nights and weekends, fixed emergency outages, missed meals with my family, holidays, birthdays... You can't just get rid of me that easily."

"Get off your high horse, man." Rickman frowned. "Some of your co-workers have been here twenty...thirty years. You're low man on this totem pole. You'll get a generous severance package...three week's pay and medical—"

Jesse straightened and slammed his fist on Rickman's desk. "That's it? Three weeks? That won't even pay my rent."

"I guess you'll have to downsize."

"I'll be damned if I let you put me out on the street."

He laughed. "I don't think you're worth three weeks...so don't look a gift horse in the mouth."

"Gift? You think that meager handout is going to

shut me up?"

"Fuck you, Curley." Rage mottled Rickman's face. "Pack your shit and get out."

"This is bullshit."

"And I want your ID badge before—"

The honk of a horn slammed him back to the present. A black Ford F-150 had pulled up beside him, so close it blocked his door from opening. The tinted window rolled down to reveal a husky, unshaven man with a neck as thick as a hydrant, slicked-back black hair, and lips blackened from chewing tobacco. "Hey there, Jesse."

Cold dread constricted his chest. He dropped the unemployment check on the passenger seat and lowered his window. "What are you doing here, Conrad?"

"That time of month...figured you'd be here to cash your unemployment check. I hope it's a doozy."

"It's peanuts, and you know it."

"Tough loss for the Yankees. I can't believe the Judge struck out three times. Kinda like you, huh? Always betting good money after bad. Time to pay up, Jesse. I'm losing patience with you."

"Give me a break, man. My luck's gonna change."

"That's what all you losers say."

Jim Keane

"You'll see. Then you're going to owe me money."

"Yeah, well, maybe so..." He spit a chaw that oozed down Jesse's car door. "But until then, how much you got?"

"I've got bills, you know, rent, gas, phone. Come see me on the second Tuesday of next week."

Conrad glowered at him. "Talk like that'll get your legs broke, boy."

"I've been scraping by on unemployment. Just give me more time to find a job."

"I don't give a hoot about your bullshit excuses." Conrad's eyes narrowed. "When you lay a bet with me, you pay your losses."

"But five grand?" He recalled the newspaper article. "I'd have to rob a bank to get that kind of money."

Conrad grumped. "It was five thousand before the Yankees game. Now, it's ten thousand. I don't care how you get it. Hell, rob a bank if you've got the balls, but I want my money by tomorrow."

"Tomorrow? You know that's not enough time."

"Then you better have some good crutches...or a wheelchair." He spat chew in through the window.

"Christ, man." Jesse swiped at the brown glob on his sleeve. "You don't scare me, besides..." He wiped his gunky hand on his jeans. "You know I'm good for it...eventually."

The thug grinned, showing his tobacco-stained teeth. "Hey. I hear your sister just graduated college." He whistled. "Man, is she a sweet piece of ass, or what?"

Jesse's heart lurched. "You stay away from her."

"What's her name? Oh, yeah. Clarissa. Maybe she'll cover your debt." He stabbed a finger at Jesse. "Pay up tomorrow, or I'll pay your sister a visit, and I promise I won't be cordial."

With a roar, Conrad's truck tore off across the parking lot.

Jesse's jaw clenched and his mouth dried at the thought of that ape manhandling Clarissa. Getting ten thousand dollars by tomorrow was imperative.

Calm down. Think about this. I could skip town. Yeah, lay low for a while 'til I get the cash. That schmuck will never find me. Oh shit. Clarissa. I can't leave her alone with that scumbag threatening her. Shit, shit, shit. I'm fucked.

In front of the bank, a man in a blue ADT shirt stood on a ladder and adjusted a camera. The bank's security system no doubt included numerous cameras, making it a bad idea to rob the place.

His phone buzzed in a text message. "*Hey, bro.*

Are we still on for lunch at the diner?"
He typed: *"See you in an hour, sis."*
"Sounds like a plan."

Jesse grabbed his unemployment check, exited, and followed the two Brinks guards into the bank. He widened his eyes at all the money they carried, sufficient to pay off Conrad and keep Clarissa safe. However, getting away with the loot created a huge conundrum.

The bank manager, a bald man with a black goatee, grey suit and suspenders, stood near the entrance and greeted the Brinks guards. "Right this way, gentlemen." He gestured toward the open vault, and the guards followed him in.

Jesse turned to the counter and handed his check to a teller through a small slot underneath the bulletproof glass. "Afternoon. I want to cash this check."

The teller, a young woman with short carrot hair and freckles, examined the check. "Do you have an account here?"

"Yes."

"I need to see some identification."

Jesse took out his wallet and handed his driver's license to the teller. She typed on the computer.

The guards and manager exited the vault. The

manager locked the wrought-iron day-gate and signed a form. "Thanks again, guys. See you next month."

The ADT technician brushed by the two exiting guards and approached the bank manager. "Cameras are operational, but the video is grainy."

The manager's eyebrows shot up. "Grainy? That's unacceptable."

"The system needs an upgrade, but I don't have the software with me."

"Go get it and come back."

"I've got other customers to see today."

"I don't care about them. I need my system working properly, and I need it now."

"Relax. I'll return tomorrow." He handed him a paper. "Here's my work order. Please sign it."

The manager scribbled on it. "You better have this fixed tomorrow."

"No problem." The ADT technician strode out.

The manager shook his head and stormed to his desk.

The teller tapped on the glass. "Mr. Curley."

"Oh, sorry. I didn't realize a bank could have so much drama."

The teller's brow creased. "I can't cash this check."

Jesse's stomach knotted. "What? Why?"

"Your account is underfunded. We require a minimum balance of fifteen hundred dollars for third-party check cashing benefits.

"It won't bounce. It's a government check. Unemployment."

"It's our policy, sir. Besides, your account is below the minimum. We've sent you several notices—"

"Look. I've been through some rough times, lost my job and can't find work."

"I understand, but we must revert your account to a standard fee-baring account."

Jesse's throat tightened. "That'll put me in the red."

The teller shrugged. "I can deposit this check in your account to prevent that."

"But I need the cash now," he shouted.

"May I suggest the check cashing place down the street?"

"But they'll keep ten percent. I can't afford that."

The manager approached. "Is there a problem here?"

The teller's face brightened. "Mr. Neary, I explained to this customer that we cannot cash this check." She waved it at him.

Jesse turned to the manager. "There must be a way to bypass this stupid rule. I've been a good customer for five years."

He cleared his throat. "Mr. Curley, if you insist on causing a scene, I must ask you to leave."

Jesse slumped his shoulders. "Please. I need this check cashed. It's nothing compared to all your cash in that vault."

"Never mind about my vault." The manager turned to the teller. "Please return Mr. Curley's check."

She slid it out through the slot. "Here you go, sir. Good luck."

He grabbed the check and stuffed it in his pocket. "This is outrageous." His embarrassment outweighed his anger.

"Is there anything else we can do for you?"

"Yeah. Go to hell."

"Have a good day, sir."

Jesse stormed toward the exit but slowed when he remembered the article. *BRONX ROBBERY NETS $200,000 IN THROUGH-THE-ROOF HEIST.* He gazed at the bank vault, the thick steel doors angled outward, the iron gate across the entrance, protecting the riches within. He assessed the distance from the front door to the vault, maybe fifteen steps, then he inspected the ceiling's typical drop design, maybe three feet of space between it and the flat roof of the one-story building.

I'll need a ladder to reach the roof, a chainsaw to cut through to the ceiling, and a rope to drop into the vault.

The manager broke him out of his planning trance. "Mr. Curley, what's the holdup? I told you to leave."

"I'm an IT guy, and I can fix your cameras, your security system, no problem. Are you hiring?"

"Sorry, we're under contract with ADT."

"That's too bad." *You're going to need them working tonight.*

He walked out whistling.

Chapter Two

After exiting the bank, Jesse scanned the rooftop and drive-thru canopy for the best access. Security cameras overlooked the front door and the pneumatic tube machines, but not the roof. A twenty-foot ladder should do the trick. He could park his car on the side road, and tree islands in the parking lot would block the view of his work from the McDonald's and the Mobil station, the only probable source of traffic late at night.

Satisfied he could pull off the heist, he drove to Universal Check Cashing on Division Street and cashed his unemployment check. Then, sitting in his car, he took out his phone and jumped online to compare prices between Walmart, Ace, and Home Depot for the cheapest telescopic ladder, chainsaw, and climbing rope. *Home Depot it is.* Though he needed the last of his cash to survive, these purchases marked an investment in a big haul.

He drove three miles to Home Depot and spotted a Peekskill Police Department cruiser parked in front, hazards flashing. A bobblehead cop waggled on the dashboard. His friend, Keith Clarkson, drove that particular car. They'd graduated from the same college...and there he stood, talking with a woman...just feet from the entrance doors.

What if he sees me buying a chainsaw, rope, and ladder? He'd say, 'Jesse, what are you doing with all that stuff? You live in a downtown apartment, not in the woods. What's going on?' 'Ah, nothing, man. I'm going to rob a bank, is all.'

Yeah, right. He parked three rows from Keith's car, kept his head down and faced away as he hurried inside.

Twenty rows of towering shelves under even taller ceilings stood before him. Directories for every department made finding what he wanted easier. Employees, dressed in jeans and orange shirts, operated cash registers and hurried through the aisles. He inhaled scents of freshly cut wood, earth from the garden shop, and stirring paint.

A sign caught his eye: THE HOME DEPOT SERVES VETERANS AND ACTIVE SERVICE MEMBERS. ENJOY 20% DISCOUNT ON ALL PURCHASES.

If only I were a veteran.

He proceeded to the tool department, outdoor power equipment, and chainsaws. Countless chainsaws lined the aisle, and he needed a quiet one.

He spotted an employee with white hair and glasses worn low on his nose. A big button on his orange apron read: HI, I'M AL. HOW CAN I HELP YOU TODAY?

Jesse pointed to three rows of chainsaws. "I'm looking for an inexpensive electric chainsaw. Something lightweight that can cut through anything."

Al rubbed his chin. "You know what you want. That's good." He stepped a little closer. "Half the bozos in this store don't have a clue."

"My neighbors complain when I'm working in the backyard, so it must be quiet."

"People like that can be annoying. Can't they?"

"They sure can, especially when I'm trying to get some work done." *Like robbing a bank.*

Al handed him a yellow chainsaw. "Check out this bad boy. The DeWalt twenty-volt battery-operated chainsaw. This'll cut through most anything and not bother the neighbors."

He grasped the handle. "Nice and lightweight." *How long will it take to cut through the bank's roof?* "How long does the battery last?"

"Two hours, my friend. You can buy yourself some spares."

I hope two hours is enough time to cut through a roof.

"Sounds great. Except... How much?"

"Buy this puppy and I'll throw in a second battery."

"Can I get your veteran's discount?"

"You serve?"

"Kabul." It was the first thing that popped into his head.

Al's eyebrows shot up. "Holy shit, son, that place was a hell hole."

"Barely got out before everything went south."

"Thank you for your service...ah..."

"Jesse. Jesse Curley."

"Jesse...okay." Al shook Jesse's hand. "My nephew served two tours in Iraq. Damn proud of that kid. I did two tours in Nam myself. Ask for the veteran's discount at checkout. Anything else?"

"A twenty-foot telescopic ladder and some rope. Fifty feet should do."

Minutes later, Jesse trundled a cart loaded with the chainsaw, ladder, and rope to the checkout counter. "I'll take the veteran's discount, please."

"A vet, huh? Thank you for your service, young man." The clerk scanned the items. "I'll need to see your VA card."

"Sure." Jesse's throat went dry. Without the

discount, he didn't have enough money...the bank heist was bust and Conrad would get up close and personal with Clarissa. He opened his wallet, and feigning a search, fumbled through the last of his money, then frowned. "I could have sworn...I'm sorry, it's not in here. I must have misplaced it. Can you take me at my word?"

"No ID, no discount. That's the rule. I'm sorry for the inconvenience."

A line had formed behind him. One man glowered with impatience. None of them knew how desperate his situation was, a matter of life and death... He spotted Al hurrying by. "Hey, Al."

He sauntered up. "What's going on, Jesse?"

"I don't have my VA card, lost it...I guess. She won't give me the discount."

"Nonsense, my boy." He looked at the clerk. "I'll vouch for him."

She shrugged and punched in a code to let the sale go through at twenty percent off.

He shook Al's hand. "Thank you, sir."

"Us vets always got each other's backs." Al hurried away.

Jesse paid the clerk in cash then hurried out to his car. Feeling like he'd dodged a howitzer shell, he stashed the ladder, rope, and chainsaw in the trunk.

He didn't see Keith or his police cruiser anywhere, so Jesse figured he was home free...until the old Corolla's engine wouldn't start. *Shit.* In his panic to get out of there, he must've pumped the gas too much. After thirty seconds, he tried again. The engine coughed, sputtered, and fired up.

Fuckin' A.

He slipped the transmission into drive and sped away, headed for the diner.

Chapter Three

Jesse's rusty Corolla chugged along the two-lane highway on Route 9 at the speed limit, leaving the Home Depot behind and heading to the Peekskill Diner, one exit north from the bank. The smell of scorching oil, the shocks banging underneath, and the engine's clatter reminded him of riding in his dad's station wagon while Clarissa and he played card games in the back.

The Hudson River glistened on his left, and boats tugged on their tethers at the marina docks. On his right, a sign read: PEEKSKILL HOMETOWN DINER. He pulled into the parking lot, ran the back of his hand across his brow, and then hurried inside. The aromas of sautéed onions frying and steak grilling greeted him. The sizzle made him ravenous. *I wish I could afford to eat here.*

Cutlery clinked as patrons ate their lunches, and kids played percussion on water glasses. At the serving window to the kitchen, a fifty-something waitress with big arms and grey hair had to yell above the din. "Hey, Carlos, where's my ham and eggs with hash browns and toast? What are you doing back there, taking a nap?"

Carlos, a muscular cook with a New York Yankees tattoo on his right arm, flipped an egg with practiced precision and wiped his brow as he read tickets clipped above the grill. He snatched up another patron's order and glared at the woman. "Don't get your panties in a wad, Thelma. It's almost ready."

Thelma folded her arms. "Tell that to the truck driver who could eat a side of beef. If you don't hurry up, you're paying for all my lost tips."

Carlos slid two fried eggs, three slices of ham, hash browns, and two pieces of buttered toast onto a plate and shoved it across the counter to Thelma. "Here you go, beautiful. One farmer's breakfast for one hungry trucker."

Thelma shook her head, snatched the breakfast, and hurried toward the truck driver's booth. "Miracles never cease."

To Jesse's left and right, two rows of ten booths stood along the walls where patrons chowed down on anything from cheeseburgers with extra fries to pancakes and sausage. Thelma hurried by him with a pot of coffee and poured the steaming brew into patrons' cups as fast as she could. She offered a warm smile for Jesse as she passed. "Get it while it's hot, sweetheart."

Jesse frowned. *I wish.*

A gaunt white-haired man with a broad nose and prominent forehead stood at the cash register near the entrance, watching the goings on. He wore a blue golf shirt that read: PEEKSKILL HOMETOWN DINER. "Hey, Jesse, are you waiting for a table?"

"Have you seen Clarissa?"

"Don't recall. Maybe I missed her."

"I'll look around. Oh...ah...Mr. Pappas, you look like you need some help. Are you hiring?"

He scoffed. "I thought you were working at Vericom. Why would you want to sling hash?"

"They laid me off."

"That's too bad. How long ago?"

"It feels like a year, but it's been six months."

Mr. Pappa's eyebrows shot up. "Christ. How you gettin' by?"

"I'm not. Unemployment's run out." Heat burned down the nape of his neck. "I'm just a number to Vericom, the odd man out."

"It defies all reason. I see Vericom's commercials touting their vast network. They must spend millions, but they can't keep their workers. What a shame."

Jesse rubbed his forehead. "I busted my ass for

the company, but in the end, they couldn't care less about me. Now, I'm just a U.S. labor statistic. Mr. Pappas, I could use a job right now...'til I can get one like I had at Vericom."

"Can't help you there. I'm scraping by as is, paying Thelma and Carlos. Both are busting their asses."

"I can wash dishes, take out the trash, or even distribute flyers."

"That's what I do around here. Sorry, Jesse. I can't afford another salary."

On the far-left booth in the corner sat a twenty-something slender blonde wearing a grey sweatshirt with large blue M-S-M-C letters across the front. She stood and waved. "Hey, Jesse."

He waved back, "There you are," and strode toward Clarissa. "I didn't see you at first. Did you have your face buried in your phone?"

Her blue eyes sparkled. "Just sent out a couple of texts. Big party tonight at the Bliss Nightclub. You should come. I'm hoping to meet someone special tonight."

"You college kids are all the same. Come here, gimme a hug."

"Ex-college kid." She extended her arms. "It's great to see you, Jesse."

"You too, sis." He gave her a big hug and then regarded her with admiration. "I can't believe it's been four years. Where's that little girl I once knew?"

"Time flies. Let's eat. I'm starving."

Thelma arrived with two cups and a coffee pot. "I hear you graduated, Clarissa."

She smiled. "Sure did. When is Mr. Pappas getting you some help?"

"Not in my lifetime. He's too busy counting his pennies." She turned to Jesse. "You find a job yet?"

He sighed. "No. Even Mr. Pappas shot me down."

"You don't wanna work in this sweatshop anyway. What can I get you?"

Clarissa put her menu on the table. "I'll take a spinach salad with grilled chicken and olive oil on the side. And that coffee sure looks good."

Thelma poured her a cup and turned to Jesse. "What about you?"

"Got any ice water?" *I can't afford anything else.*

Clarissa brushed Jesse's hand. "Get whatever you want. I've got you covered. At least have a cup of coffee."

"Alright." He pulled his hand away. "Salad, huh? I thought you were a cheeseburger kind of girl."

"My roommate got me into eating healthy."

Thelma filled a cup for Jesse. "I'll put in that salad order. Gotta keep Carlos on his toes." She smirked and left.

Clarissa fanned her cup with her hand. "I'm sorry you still haven't found work."

"It sucks. I've had interviews with T-Mobile, AT&T, and even Cricket Wireless, but no luck."

"Something will turn up."

Something has. "I might have a side job tonight."

Her eyebrows rose. "What kind of job?"

He sipped hazelnut-scented coffee as he concocted a vague answer. "Pays cash...off the books."

"Stripping? Prostitution?"

He grumped. "Nothing that exciting."

"Then what?"

"I don't want to jinx myself." He made a zipper motion across his lips.

Clarissa's brow creased as her blue eyes probed his face. "Why the mystery? I'm your sister. You can tell me."

He glanced out the window, contemplating his piss-poor luck. A police cruiser sped by. He thought about returning the stuff to Home Depot, spare himself a ride in a squad car to prison. "Enough about me. How was college? Do you have a job lined up?"

"Don't change the subject. Does it have anything to do with gambling? You're not very good at it."

"It's nothing like that."

"Be careful, Jesse, whatever you're doing. I'm worried about you."

"I can take care of myself. Now tell me about college."

"It was awesome. Made friends, learned a lot and made contacts after an internship at Microsoft." Her face brightened. "They want to hire me as a software engineer in the fall."

"That's great. I'm proud you could find a job so fast."

"I guess because I'm younger than you."

"Yeah. I'm an old cow been put out to pasture."

"Moo," she quipped.

Thelma returned. "Here's your salad with lots of grilled chicken and olive oil. Hope you like it."

"It looks great, Thelma, thanks. Jesse, what about you?"

"I'm good." He stirred his coffee, wondering if he should abandon his plans to rob the bank. As he glanced at Clarissa, Conrad's ugly mug intruded. What choice did he have? He couldn't let him get his grubby mitts on her.

Thelma topped off their coffees. "I'll come back

later."

"Jesse, you seem so distant."

He clasped his hands and interlaced his fingers. "I just can't get a break. At this rate, I'll soon be homeless and on the streets."

"You can stay with Mom and me, sleep on the couch."

"I won't impose on you guys. How's Mom, anyway? I haven't spoken to her in a while."

"She's down in Florida with Uncle Francis. You're welcome to stay with us. It's no problem. Besides, Mom could use a man around the house...since..." Her voice wavered; tears shined in her eyes. "I miss Dad."

Jesse squeezed her hand. "I miss him too. Dad was a great guy."

Chapter Four

L ater that night, inside the Bliss Nightclub on the outskirts of Peekskill, Clarissa Curley be-bopped onto the dance floor and probed the vibrant crowd for a hookup. She wore a loose black mini, cross-your-heart red halter, sheer, smooth stockings, and peek-a-boo toe high heels. Gold jewelry tied it all together: chain necklace, band bracelets, and hoop earrings. Yes, she was the queen of the Bliss, and everyone paid homage with jealous and lustful eyes watching her every move.

Speakers boomed. Multi-colored strobe lights pulsed. Bosomy servers with LED-lighted trays stalked around the bar and nearby tables, hocking drinks. Bartenders hustled to prepare shots of Jamesons for waiting patrons lined up between barstools.

The DJ, sporting sunglasses, baggy clothes from the hood, and a Yankee cap on backward, cut records from disco to rap. Between spins he announced, "Yo, my peeps. Last call is coming soon. Order up before it's too late. Here's one from the Bee Gees."

Clarissa downed her vodka tonic and left the glass on a nearby table. She swayed to the beat of Stayin' Alive.

Full of muscles and attitude, a jock and recent college graduate like herself, Tommy Jackson, approached her, pushing his black hair out of his eyes and bopping to the beat.

Clarissa's heart raced. This night might not be a total bust, after all.

Tommy bumped and grinded against her. She didn't resist. Instead, with her hands on her hips, she beckoned him with hip thrusts and a wink. He wrapped his arms around her. Strobe lights flashed, and the club reverberated with old-time disco music. She melted in his arms, hugged him and kissed him. "We did it, Tommy." She had to shout over the music. "No more grueling schedules, running to classes, cramming for finals."

"It feels great to be free," he whispered in her ear. "B-T-W. You look amazing."

Damn, he's hot. Tight jeans, sleeveless shirt, biceps and abs galore. Her breathing quickened. "Where have you been all night?"

"Around."

She flowed with the music. The club's atmosphere transported her to a fantasy world where pleasure reigned supreme, and she'd had just enough to drink to prove it. She ran her fingers through his long hair. "Tommy, I need this break after four years of kicking ass in college."

"Any job prospects?"

"I'm working at Microsoft this fall as a software engineer. My internship paid off."

Jump Around by House of Pain blasted from the speakers.

Tommy pumped his fists. "I love this song. Come on, Clarissa, jump around." He jumped every time Everlast and his band shouted, *"Jump Around! Jump Around! Jump up and get down!"*

Clarissa timed her jumps with Tommy's. Her heart hammered. God, it's great to be free. Free of school. Go anywhere. I can do anything I want, starting with Tommy.

He unbuttoned his shirt. Clarissa licked her lips at the sight of his chiseled abs.

The song ended, and the DJ cut into a hip-hop song, Poison, by Bell Biv DeVoe.

She wrapped her arms around him. He kissed her hard. Her face flushed. She leaned forward. "Let's go outside and see the stars."

Hand-in-hand, he led her through the crowd, dodging dancers. Bell Biv DeVoe sang: "That girl is poison." His nearness made her palms sweat, cheeks flush, and heart race. We're finally going to do it. Yes!

She gripped his hand tighter as he led her out the club's front door. Cool air filled her lungs. A jacked bouncer wearing a black shirt and jeans stood there, arms folded like Superman. Crushed cigarette butts smoldered on the ground at his feet. Twenty yards ahead, cars jammed the club's parking lot. She stood with Tommy under the neon-lit marquee and squinted at the bright lights. "It's too bright here. Let's go around back where it's dark enough to stargaze."

"Great idea." He gripped her hand and led her through a passageway toward the alley behind the club. The Bliss Nightclub skirted the eight-foot-wide walkway on the right, and an old industrial building with cracked brick walls rose on the left. As they walked, the steady pump of the club faded.

A sickle-shaped moon shined its romantic light into the otherwise gloomy alley where, next to a trash bin, garbage bags were lined up like dead soldiers. Shards of broken bottles lay scattered on the ground. She recoiled at the stench of urine and pulled away from his grip and lit out at a full run.

"Hey. Where are you going?"

Her heart thumped as she dashed toward the

woods beyond the club. The dirt road was hell to navigate in high heels. "Catch me if you can."

"Hey, wait."

She dashed around a tree, leaned against the rough bark, and inhaled gasping breaths. Moonlight dappled down through the high branches. He'd better hurry up. It's spooky out here. The dirt road, lined with trees, led to the main highway into Peekskill.

There's no way he can get lost.

Sure enough, Tommy's footsteps pounded in the dirt toward her.

She let out a giggle.

He pivoted to the sound, rounded the tree, and locked eyes with her. "There you are."

She smiled. "I've been waiting for you. What took you so long?"

"Aren't you full of surprises."

"What are you going to do about it?"

He nuzzled in close. "I've been looking forward to this."

"Me too." She pulled his already unbuttoned shirt down off his shoulders, the distant music thumping, as was her pounding heart.

He pinned her against the tree, his mouth finding hers in the moonlight. In a frantic flurry, her tongue found his, and they kissed with reckless abandon, each tongue probing and tasting the other in search of passion's highway to heaven. She stole wanton breaths between their heated lips.

He slipped his hands under her blouse and caressed her breasts, lighting her libido on fire. As the rough bark dug into the soft flesh of her back, she wished, for a fleeting moment, they were in her dorm room, ravaging each other under crisp sheets as they'd done in their good-old college days.

"Oh, Tommy. Don't stop."

"It's been so long."

A horn blared from the alley.

She jumped. Through the trees she could see blinding headlights as she clung to Tommy, hoping it wasn't the police. How embarrassing would that be?

"Oh, shit." He backed off, pulled down her blouse, and put on his shirt. "It's my dad."

"Your dad? W-T-F?"

"I forgot about work." With trembling fingers, he buttoned the shirt. "I have to be up early. Come on." He led her back to the alley, leisurely, as if they'd been on an innocent stroll.

"Tommy." His stout dad jumped from a radically lifted pickup truck. He could have been a lumberjack in that checkered flannel shirt, jeans, and black cap. "Get your ass over here."

"Relax, Dad. I'm coming."

"Who's that girl you're with?"

"My friend Clarissa."

"She better not end up pregnant, boy."

"Come on, Dad. It's nothing like that."

Not tonight, anyway. She waved at him timidly. "Why is he so angry?"

"He's a control freak. Let's hang out soon." He kissed her quick.

"And you, young lady, you should be at home." He stabbed a finger at her. "It's not safe to be out this late at night."

Her cheeks burned with embarrassment. "Thank you, sir."

Tommy hurried to his dad's truck.

"Text me," Clarissa said.

Tommy stopped and looked at her, but before he could reply, his dad slapped him on the head. "Get in."

The door slammed, and the truck skidded away, leaving her alone in the alley. She shivered and straightened her disheveled blouse. I'll see him again.

As she approached the back of the club, hip-hop music pounded through the walls. She hurried toward the passageway that led to the club's front door, but before she reached it, behind her, the crunching of glass quickened and startled her. Heart hammering, she whirled to see a tall figure looming in the gloom. The stranger wore a 7-11 mask and clutched a Dundee knife that glinted in the moonlight.

Chapter Five

Rory O'Rourke parked his cab in front of the Bliss around 2:00 a.m., poised for the club's revelers to emerge. Drunk and hungry patrons fancied late-night diners or after-hours joints, and he aimed to cater to their needs. He'd be the first in line to fetch them. After arriving from Ireland, he'd earned his green card and hack license last year—ah, the American dream.

Tis a great country. Americans are always happy when they get into the cab. Always generous with their tips.

If he hustled, he could get a couple of trips from the club to various destinations. It wasn't a big deal if they snuck a few drinks into the cab. Not at all. Whatever made the Yanks happy. He exited the car, leaned against the front fender, pulled the stubby bill of his green tweed cap low on his forehead, and waited for the partygoers to exit the club.

***

At the sight of the gigantic, knife-toting masked man looming in the moonlight, Clarissa froze in terror, and a chill raced down her spine. She backpedaled, her stomach clenching with each step.

The man stalked toward her with a sinister, determined stride, and his presence cast an eerily long and unnatural shadow down the alley.

Run, girl. Get the hell out of here.

She whirled, bolted toward the passageway, and screamed, "Help. Help."

However, the man, moving with bounding strides, overtook her, seized her arm, and hurled her toward the trash bin and line of garbage bags. She struck the ground, hands first, slicing her palms on shards of broken beer bottles and shattered glass. Pain screamed up her arms. She cringed at the sight of her blood dripping on the ground.

Fighting panic and the instinct to flee, as he'd only catch her again, she had no other choice but to fight. As the man's heavy footsteps approached, she reached for the neck of a broken beer bottle, levered herself to her feet, and brandished the jagged weapon. "Stay away from me."

The bastard clasped the knife, blocking her escape from the alley, and stopped, his head tilted, as if awaiting her next move.

She blinked back tears and held her chin high. *I'll survive this somehow.* She struggled to swallow, her throat was that tight. She screamed, but only a squeak came out. Just as well, the blaring music drowned out her cries. With her free hand, she grabbed a garbage bag and hurled it at her attacker. He batted it aside, and as he stepped forward, she raised the jagged bottle neck. "I'll cut you, motherfucker."

He lunged at her, slugged her in the jaw with a sledgehammer fist. Moonlight turned black, and she hit the alley floor again. The coppery taste of blood erupted in her mouth. Battered, she lay there shaking. Her attacker towered over her.

He can't win, he just can't...or I'll never see Tommy again.

She rolled to her side and slashed out with the beer bottle, slicing into his pant leg. The man groaned and jumped back, giving her a split second to regain her feet, and leaving her heels behind, she dashed for the passageway.

Come on, girl. You can make it. Don't give up. You'll survive.

Fire exploded in her feet as the glass shards made hamburger of her soles. She stumbled. She screamed, primeval in the way it came out this time, as a small animal clamped in the jaws of a beast. The assailant tackled her and slammed her to the ground. Her face took the brunt of the impact. Blinding pain shot through her nose, mouth, jaw, and skull.

He flipped her over, knelt on her neck, and brought the blade down. She knew it stabbed her chest. She knew it stabbed her stomach. She knew the sharp edge sliced into her leg. Oddly, she felt no pain, but pressure...and cold, so cold.

***

Rory stood outside his cab, leaning on the front fender, awaiting a flood of patrons to pour from the club doors at closing time. From somewhere in the distance came a high-pitched scream, animalistic in its intensity, but a woman's scream, for sure. It sent shivers down his spine, and the hairs on the nape of his neck prickled. He tossed his green cap on the front seat and raced toward the sound, perhaps in the woods behind the club. His hurried steps slowed at the dark and narrow walkway between the buildings, his senses on high alert as he stalked toward the back alley. "Hey. What the hell is going on back there?"

When he cleared the corner of the wall, he saw a giant son of a bitch on top of a woman...stabbing her with a knife. Disbelief gripped him. What in God's name? Rory's pulse thundered in his throat. He had no weapons, just his bare fists, which had won him a few boxing matches and bar brawls, and without a second thought, he bolted toward the fray. "Stop.

Stop."

In the middle of the alley, the masked attacker had orchestrated a bloodbath. He looked up at the sudden interruption, held the bloody blade high, hesitating to deliver another blow as if to assess the new and unexpected situation.

"You better get out of here, arsehole."

He stood, a tower of a beast above the still woman, then fled down the dirt road into the woods. Seconds later, tires screeched, and engine roaring, a vehicle peeled away, the sounds fading into the night.

Rory knelt beside the bleeding woman, slumped among the glass shards and litter. What a disgusting place to die. The night stank of blood and urine, and he gagged on the vile stench. He fumbled with his phone to turn on the flashlight light app. Disheveled flaxen hair framed a battered face. Spatters of blood trailed from a pair of high heels lying helter-skelter in the dirt and on down the alley to the red pool in which she now lay.

What a fierce struggle the lass put up.

He gaped at her face and surveyed the extent of her injuries. "Jaysus. Why did that muckie do this to you?"

She gasped, and bloody bubbles leaked from her nose. Knife wounds pocked her blood-soaked blouse, her face was slashed, and a meaty gash in her thigh pumped a streamer, probably from her femoral artery.

He had to stop the bleeding, but where would he start with all the wounds to choose from? The streamer seemed to be the most life-threatening, though he was sure she'd suffered a collapsed lung, among other debilitating lacerations to her internals.

Determined to save her, he dropped the phone and pressed his right hand on the open leg wound; blood oozed out between his fingers. He pressed his left hand on the worst of her facial injuries, a gash in her forehead.

She's alive, thank the Lord, but no telling fer how long.

"Somebody call 911."

Chapter Six

Jesse parked on the side street near the vacant Apple Farm Commons parking lot, close to the bank, but not close enough to get picked up on video. He retrieved the chainsaw, ladder, and rope from the trunk, set them on the ground, then donned a balaclava and gloves. Before he could tote his gear to the bank, his cell phone rang. He removed a glove and fetched the phone from his pocket. The display read *Peekskill Police Department*. Startled, he widened his eyes and opened his mouth; his mind raced with apprehension.

Why are the police calling me now?

Suddenly, lights flashed from an approaching car.

A fast river of hot adrenaline rushed through him. He gathered his equipment and shoved it back into the trunk. Phone still ringing like an irritable child, he scrambled into the back seat and ducked under the old blanket. His breath came out in spurts and his heart thwacked his sternum. He ripped off his balaclava and gloves.

Did the driver see me?

Prison seemed a real possibility. He quietly answered the ringing phone. "Yeah."

"Jesse?" Officer Keith Clarkson said.

"Hey, Keith." He hoped to sound nonchalant. "What's up?"

"Your...Sister..."

"My sister?"

"Clarissa." His voice rasped. "She's hurt."

"Hurt? How?" His stomach lurched. "What happened?"

"She's...in the hospital, Jess."

He gripped the phone tighter. "What? The hospital? What happened to her, damn it?"

The approaching car pulled up behind Jesse's car, and its headlights shined in through the rear window.

"They found her...Jess, I shouldn't tell you over the phone."

Fear shuddered through his bones. "Found her? Where?"

A door opened and shut. Someone had exited the car, and now a beam of light shined on the blanket and swept around inside the car.

Jesse held his breath.

"It's bad," Keith said.

An icy hand clutched Jesse's heart. What was so bad that a cop couldn't tell him? "Where is she?" he whispered.

"Why are you whispering?"

A tapping sounded on the window. "Hey." The voice outside was gruff. "You can't sleep here?" The light held steady on the blanket.

Jesse didn't move a muscle. *Go away, goddamnit.*

"Jesse, are you there?"

"This car better be gone when I come around again, or I'll have it towed. Piece of junk."

The light went away. Footsteps tromped to the car behind him. A door opened and closed, and the car pulled out around him and drove off.

Jesse exhaled, shot up, and peeked out the windshield in time to see a private security car turn into the parking lot, big phony badge on the door, amber light on the roof blinking. Shit. *I hadn't factored that guy into my plans.* It was a damn stroke of good luck that Keith had called. "What the hell happened to Clarissa?"

"She got cut up pretty bad."

"Jesus Christ." Conrad must've gotten to her...but it's not tomorrow yet..well...technically it was, at two o'clock in the morning. "What the fuck? Somebody attacked her?"

"Behind the Bliss."

The car's interior seemed to close in on him, crushing him...threatening to crumble his sanity into molecular dust. He clambered into the driver's seat.

"Keith, what hospital?" he shouted into the phone.

"Hudson Valley on Crompond Road."

"I'll meet you there."

"No. I just got a call about a suspicious car near the Peekskill bank."

Goosebumps prickled down his spine. And if that wasn't bad enough, the security car came back around the corner, slowly, like the grim reaper was driving. *Shit.* "Gotta go." He hung up and cranked the ignition, but the engine wouldn't start. *Not now. No, not now.* He slammed the flat of his hands on the wheel. *What else can go wrong?* He tried again, this time pressing the gas pedal to the floor. The engine sputtered and caught. Damn carburetor had flooded the engine again. He made a mental note to get that fixed. *Oh, right. I don't have any money.*

The security car passed by, slow enough for the guard to make eye contact with him. Jesse waved like everything was honky dory then pulled out behind him. The guard turned right into the parking lot. Jesse drove down the block to McDonald's, where he flipped a U-turn and headed east on Welcher to the ramp for northbound Highway 9. The hospital was less than two miles away. He stayed within the 45mph speed limit, though his foot itched to floor the gas. Angst about his sister tortured him. How bad? *Will she live or die?*

He thought their mother should know about this emergency, pulled her up on his phone. It rang several times. *Come on, Mom, pick up.*

"Hello?"

"Hey, Mom. Sorry to wake you."

"Jesse? Do you know what time it is? Are you in trouble again?"

"Mom, would you listen to me?"

"I have no more money for you. Take care of yourself, for once. With your father gone, money is tight. If you're in jail—"

"Jesus, Mom. It's about Clarissa."

"Clarissa? I'm so proud of her, graduating from college and all. She was always such a party girl—"

"Mom, someone attacked her."

"Attacked? Dear God. My baby girl. Is she okay?"

"I don't know. She's at the hospital. I'm going there now. I think you should come back."

"Oh, my baby." Her voice was shrill. "Oh, my God."

"I'm sorry to ruin your vacation with Uncle Francis, but you need to be here."

"We'll be on the next flight. Call me when you hear something more."

"I will. I love you."

The call ended, and Jesse sped on toward the hospital.

Chapter Seven

Twenty minutes after the 911 call, Detective Harry Kellerman arrived on the scene of the assault behind the Bliss Nightclub. A crowd of onlookers had gathered. He slapped on latex gloves, and flashlight in hand, he got out of his unmarked black Tahoe and hustled toward the crime scene. A chilly predawn wind off the Hudson River cut through his black slacks, and his black boots crunched dirt and glass shards as he proceeded down the alley. He wished he'd worn a heavy coat, rather than this blue jacket with PEEKSKILL POLICE DEPARTMENT lettering on the back.

A blue on white Peekskill police cruiser was parked diagonally across the alley, its misery lights flashing. Yellow police tape, thrashing in the wind, cordoned off the crime scene.

Approaching the tape, he encountered a plump police officer with puffy cheeks mottled by the chill. His nameplate read NORRIS. "Hold up there, sir."

Kellerman flashed his badge. "I'm the detective on this case. Kellerman. Lieutenant Harry

Kellerman."

"Ah...the new dick from the NYPD. Welcome to Peekskill. I hear Detective Doherty is on vacation. Left you with the short straw on this one."

"Yeah. Lucky me."

"We used to be a peaceful small town...until this."

The iron-tinted stench of blood permeated the air.

"What do you got, Norris?"

He consulted a note pad. "The vic is Clarissa Curley. Peekskill native, twenty-two, college grad."

"Is she dead?"

"She was sliced up pretty bad."

"But she's not dead?"

"EMTs rushed her to Hudson Valley ER with multiple stab wounds."

"Damn lucky, huh?"

"She was attacked in an alley, sir. Don't sound like *lucky* to me.

Kellerman shook his head and peered over Norris's shoulder. The club's alley light dimly illuminated the area. Blood had pooled on the ground in two places, and a trail led to a pair of high heel shoes lying askew in the dirt amid the garbage and broken glass. He surveyed the alley, the dirt road, the woods, and asked the obvious question. "What the hell was she doing back here?"

"It's spooky, sir. She was dressed to the nines, probably a patron, maybe drunk, who knows?"

"Any witnesses?"

"A cabbie, ah..." He referred to his notes. "Rory O'Rourke saw the guy stabbing her. Big guy, he says, wearing a mask, escaped down the alley and into the woods. I had a squad take him to the station to give us an official statement."

"Good call." These small-town cops knew the drill. *Just what I need.*

"Where's CSI?"

"On the way."

"Cameras?"

"Yes, sir." Norris turned and pointed to the club's rear wall. "There's one. The bouncer told me the owner would have the video, if there is any."

"Let's hope it's working." He ducked under the police tape, turned on his flashlight, and approached the largest pool of blood. Paramedics' litter was scattered about the area where her body had lain: blood-soaked pads, discarded plastic bags, strips of cloth bandages, everything left over from what must've been a frantic attempt to save her life.

The high-heel shoes were about eight steps from

where she'd fallen. A jagged bottle neck glinted in the light beam; its sharp edge appeared to be coated with coagulated blood. He stepped to it, knelt, picked it up, gave it a closer look under the flashlight beam. *That's blood alright.* He stood and slipped the bottleneck into his jacket pocket. She'd put up one hell of a fight. If not for the witness, she certainly would have died right here at the scene. He didn't have time to finish the job.

CSI has a lot of work to do.

He shined the light across the trash bin and line of garbage bags to assess what CSI would find. One was upended off to the side. Most were spattered with blood, castoff drops, it appeared, from a flailing blade, and then he swept the beam to a passageway between the club and the next building. Judging from the way the crime scene elements lined up, he knew she was trying to get to the narrow path to escape him. He followed the scuffed dirt and disturbed glass shards to the passage, then stalked between the high walls to the brightly lit sidewalk and marquee in front of the club. She'd chosen darkness over light. Foolish girl.

Wondering if anyone had seen her leave, he stepped inside the nightclub, all lit up real bright. The DJ was dismantling his booth, barmaids were turning chairs upside-down on tables, and the bartender was polishing his workspace. A bouncer-type-guy, muscular in a black wife–beater T, sleeve tats, and all puffy-chested, immediately confronted him. "Hey, we're closed, mister."

Kellerman showed him his badge, and the bouncer deflated, didn't look so tough anymore. "Did you see the girl walk out, the one in the alley, all sliced up like deli meat?"

"No, sir. I was busy corralling a troublesome drunk. When I kicked him out was the first time I heard about her, some guy yelling, 'Call 911.' Beats me why she was back there. Not my fault, man."

"Does the security camera work, the one above the back door?"

"I believe so, but like I told the other cop, only the owner can access the video."

"You don't say. Alley cameras rarely ever work."

"Mr. Fortune should be here come 9:00 a.m."

"I'll be back then." He exited the club, stalked the passageway around back to the alley, and got there just as another police car arrived, white and blue lights flashing from the windshield. He strode Officer Norris. "Who the hell is that coming late to this party?"

"You're going to love this guy, sir."

Jim Keane

A slender, bespectacled man stepped out of an antiquated Crown Victoria cruiser. He appeared to be in his thirties, red hair, and wearing a jacket like Kellerman's. "Sorry, I'm late, fellas. Busy night. Just finished up a DUI accident. What a mess." He nodded to the cop. "Mornin', John."

"Detective Kellerman, this is Chuck Thompson with CSI."

"Hey, you're the new guy, right?" Thompson shook Kellerman's hand. "New York City's finest, yes sir, NYPD. Welcome to the armpit of the Hudson River."

"It's a big change from the big city."

Chuck grinned. "You'll get used to the sticks."

"Where's your team?"

"The van is on the way. What happened here?"

"Girl got cut up bad," Norris said. "Some psychopath. The crime scene is all yours."

Kellerman stepped back. "If you come up with something I can use to nail a suspect, contact me first."

"I'll take some pictures, collect samples of everything, blood and fibers. Kinda reminds you of back home, huh, detective?" He laughed.

"That's not funny, Chuck. Get busy."

"Whoa." Thompson looked at Norris. "Touchy

fucker, huh."

Norris shrugged. "Don't push it."

Kellerman stormed to his Tahoe. "I'm headed to the station to interview the witness."

***

Kellerman raced the two miles to the Police Station, wondering just how much the witness had seen, whether or not he could ID the masked man. He parked in the south lot, rushed around the corner of the brick building, and bounded down the steps to the entrance door. As he traversed the lobby, he greeted the sergeant at the duty desk, a gruff man with streaks of grey running through his black hair. "My witness still here?"

"Interview room one." He saluted with his coffee mug.

"Better make a full pot of that brew, Sarge."

Notepad in hand, Kellerman hustled into the interview room and closed the door. "Sorry to keep you waiting."

"What took you so long?" The cabbie, a husky man, removed his green cap, loosing curls of brown hair. He sat on a swivel chair beside a small table. Dried blood coated his hands and smeared his shirt and face. "Me cab's sitting out front of the Bliss, making me squat toward the American Dream."

Jim Keane

Kellerman pulled up a chair of his own. "Don't we all have to sacrifice something to do our civic duty? It's been a long night, and we're all tired. Thanks for coming down here...ah..." he consulted his notepad, "Rory, is it?"

"Rory O'Rourke. Born and bred Irish. Got me green card, if ya wanna see it."

"I'm Detective Kellerman. Now tell me, O'Rourke, what's with all the blood on you?"

"I heard her scream, tried to help her, put pressure on the worst of her wounds. That's where the blood come from."

"And the knife? What did you do with the knife?"

"You must have me confused with someone else."

"Everyone is a suspect until I know different. Besides, you've just admitted that blood on your hands is hers."

"How's the poor lass doing?"

"Why would you care? You tried to kill her."

"Is this going to take all night?"

Kellerman grumped. "I've got some coffee coming."

"A we bit of tea would be nice."

"Forget it. Water?"

"I just want to return to me cab, so let's get on with it."

"I'll be as quick as I can. Should I talk to your boss, explain that you're a suspect in an assault?"

"I am me own boss, man. It's the American way. And you keep accusing me of stabbing that lass, I'll ask for a lawyer. That too is the American way."

"Okay. Let's start with how you got involved in this mess."

"I am waiting for the club to close, hustle a fare or two, when I heard her scream. Went running, don't know why, but I did, ran around back to the alley. Can't never unsee what I seen."

"What did you see?"

"Oh, I seen your man stabbing the poor lass, alright."

"Can you describe the man?"

Rory's brow creased. "No telling, he wore a mask, big guy, like you, linebacker type, taller than me, for sure. Dressed heavy, big coat, baggy, jeans, too, you know."

"How much do you think he weighed?"

"I don't know for sure."

"What did he do when you saw him?"

"He stopped, had that blade in the air, ready for another go at her, but he froze, maybe 'cause I told him to stop."

"Told him?"

"I was yelling at him to stop, and he did. Damnedest thing. But she wasn't moving. Maybe he was done...ran like a rabbit, he did. Down the alley and into the woods."

"What did you do next?"

"I checked to see if the poor lass was alive." He held up his hands. "So much blood."

"Did you see him throw anything as he ran, the knife, a glove, her purse, maybe?"

"Not that I could see."

Knuckles rapped on the door. It opened. A cop delivered coffee in two Styrofoam cups. Kellerman took both, set them on the table. "Thanks, Sarge."

The door closed.

Rory sniffed. "Who would do such a thing?"

"That's what we're here to find out...how much you saw, what you might know. How involved you are. Is there anything else you can remember? His voice? Did he say anything?"

"Nothin'."

"His eyes? Could you see what color —?"

"Too dark."

"A vehicle, a car, a truck..?"

"Loud. I heard it drive away from somewhere in

the woods. Maybe his. Maybe not."

Kellerman closed his notebook. "You're not much help, you know. You didn't see the guy's face. I can't show you a line-up. You've given me nothing we can use in court."

"You gotta find him, detective. He's out there, and he can attack again. Nobody is safe in Peekskill until you do."

"You think I don't know that?"

"Sorry. I'm scared." He stood. "I hope the lass don't die."

"See the Sergeant out front. He'll get you a ride back to your cab."

The door closed. Kellerman stared at the coffee cups, still steaming. "Fuck." He swiped the cups off the table, flinging coffee everywhere.

Chapter Eight

Fit to be tied, Jesse arrived at the hospital. He drove directly to the emergency entrance, but before he could park, hc had to wait for EMTs to push a gurney from an ambulance and into the building. This early in the morning, there were several open spaces, so after the ambulance moved, he claimed one closest to the doors. After stashing the balaclava and gloves in the trunk with the chainsaw, rope, and ladder, he rushed into the ER.

"I need to see my sister," he said to the woman at the counter, an administrative type, hair up in a bun and wearing a green blazer.

"Who is your sister?"

"Clarissa Curley. I hear she's in ICU. I have to see her."

"It's way past visiting hours. You'll have to come back between 11 a.m. and 6 p.m."

"Is there any chance you can bend the rules?"

"I'm sorry, I can't."

Her phone rang. She picked up, listened, then examined her computer monitor. "There's a

Small Town Killer

gentleman here asking about her now." She looked at him. "Are you Jesse Curley?"

"Yes. That's me." Hope bloomed in his heart.

She hung up. "Wait here. The police want a word with you."

"Huh?"

A squad car skidded up out front. Jesse, now confused, turned to see Officer Keith Clarkson bail out and hurry in through the sliding glass doors. His duty blues were sharply pressed as if fresh from the closet. "Jesse," he shouted as he paced toward him.

"She won't let me in to see Clarissa." He indicated the stoic woman.

Keith removed his duty cap. "Five minutes," he said to her. "What harm could it do?"

"You know the rules, officer. Visiting hours only."

"She might not make it 'til then. She's his sister, man. Have a heart, will you...please?"

The woman peered around. "Okay. ICU is on the third floor, but don't make a sound. Sick folks are trying to sleep."

Nobody gets any sleep in a hospital... "Thanks." Jesse followed Keith down the hall to a bank of elevators where he frantically punched the UP button and waited. And waited. "To hell with this." He shoved open the door to the stairwell and stormed up the steps, taking two at a time, his footfalls echoing back from the cold concrete walls.

Keith loped up behind him. "What's the hurry, Jess? She's not going anywhere?"

"You said she might not make it...to visiting hours." The climb was already stealing his breath.

"Hey, it got us in, didn't it?"

"She's cut up pretty bad. Was that a lie, too?" He reached the third floor and flung open the door.

Keith grabbed Jesse's shoulder and spun him around. "Slow down," he said in a gruff whisper. "Get your shit together, man. Relax, or you'll get us tossed out of here."

Jesse scowled. "I don't want to be here...I don't want none of this, but thanks for your help."

"So go easy."

"Yeah. Easy." He grabbed a deep breath.

At the end of the hallway stood a set of double doors marked ICU. On the right, a nurse sat behind a counter lined with computer monitors, and on the back wall, video screens displayed night-vision images of the ward beyond the doors. This early in the morning, she must've been the backbone of the skeleton crew on duty. She sipped coffee from a mug.

Jesse rushed to her. "I need to see my sister."

The nurse set down her mug, regarded him, glanced at Keith, and frowned. "You guys shouldn't be up here. Visiting hours start at eleven—"

"She might not make it 'til then." *Worked once, so what the hell?*

"Who's your sister?"

"Clarissa Curley."

"Oh dear. Her? She's in critical condition. ER treated her for a collapsed lung, got the bleeding stopped. Took six pints of blood to bring back her color. Surgeons patched up her lacerated liver and intestines. She's scheduled for a second surgery at 10 a.m., to remove glass from her feet, as long as she remains stable."

"Can I see her, please?"

"You don't want to see her like this. Trust me. Besides, she's in a drug-induced coma. She won't even know you're there."

"Just a couple minutes. We'll be quiet. I swear."

"Please," Keith put in.

"Alright. Two minutes." She pressed a button on the counter. The double doors whirred and angled open. "Second bed on the right. Don't touch anything."

Keith followed Jesse into the ICU ward. The air reeked of disinfectant. Curtained bays lined each wall, left and right, each numbered with a black-on-white sign. On the far wall, a door marked EXIT probably opened to the operating rooms and the innards of Hudson Valley Hospital. He stepped to curtain number two.

"I'll wait here," Keith whispered.

As Jesse entered Clarissa's bay, he was unprepared for what he saw. A cluster of machines surrounded a bed, eerily quiet, with blinking lights and monitors that displayed rows of oscillating lines in different colors, life's electronic signature playing out in real time. A mass of hoses and wires reached to a recumbent form on the bed, which by no means resembled a human, much less Clarissa, bandaged and masked beyond recognition. Even her feet were wrapped.

Denial became his first line of defense against the horror laid out before him. "Oh my God," he muttered. *This can't be happening. It can't be real.*

Then common sense prevailed, the true reality of her situation. *She's dead. Those machines are just keeping her alive until they pull the plug. The mortician will prepare papers for Mom to sign. The order will say 'do not resuscitate.' There's nothing I can do...*

Conrad's threat had become very real. He'd found her, and he killed her...*because of me. I made the*

Small Town Killer

bets. I lost. I owed the money, but that son of bitch didn't have to go and do this to her. For that, I'm gonna kill him. Tie him up with rope and cut him up with a chainsaw, an arm, a leg, a piece at a time. He's going to pay with blood and pain.

He stepped back from behind the curtain, felt a hand on his shoulder. "Keith, I just had lunch with her yesterday. Where's the fun-loving girl who had so much promise? She isn't living. She's dying." He couldn't tell him what Conrad had said. The threat. Jesse wanted him all to himself, but for show he said, "Who could have done this?" Tears burned in his eyes.

"The detective on the case is doing everything he can. You have to give him time to sort it all out."

"This makes no sense." Truthfully, it made perfect sense. He had to get to Conrad before the detective figured out the who-done-it and why.

He exited the hospital while the maddening clamor of guilt and revenge reverberated through his mind. Panic set in. Gasping for air, he felt his heart rate jump to the outer limits. "I've gotta go."

Keith clapped a hand on Jesse's arm. "The sun will be up soon. Let's get some coffee, have a chat."

He pulled away. "Fuck the coffee. You've got a monster to catch."

"Will you calm down? I have to talk to you."

"I need to get out of here. Get my mind straight. All I see is Clarissa's unspeakable condition." He headed toward his car.

Keith grabbed his arm again, this time with authority, whipped him around, and slammed him against the trunk of his patrol car.

"What the hell, Keith?"

"I'm not fooling around with you, Jess. Where were you earlier this morning?"

"Let go of me."

"Not until you tell me what's going on."

"What are you talking about?" Jesse played dumb, but he knew there was only one reason Keith would be asking him that question. He'd investigated the suspicious car, talked to the security guard who'd given him the Corolla's plate number...

"Why the hell was your car parked on Welcher at 2 a.m.?"

His stomach roiled. "It's a free country."

"Answer my question. What are you up to?"

"Keith, you know me."

"I know you're unemployed, broke, most likely. You've got something up your sleeve. I'm telling you, whatever it is, forget it."

"Keith, you're treating me like a criminal when

some maniac assaulted my sister."

"I'm trying to keep you out of trouble here."

"What do you want me to say? I was going to rob the bank?"

"Were you?"

"Come on, man. Me? Rob a bank? That's crazy talk. I stopped for a burger at McDonald's. Is that a crime these days?"

"You parked two blocks away."

"I like to walk late at night."

"The security guard swears he thwarted a bank robbery."

"He's delusional."

"I know you're hurting. Times are tough. Don't do anything stupid." He let go of Jesse's arm.

"You should be more worried about finding the guy who attacked my sister."

"The detective wants to see you tomorrow, down at the station—"

"Me? Why?"

"For questioning...about Clarissa. You might know something you don't realize you know."

"I know she was going out...to the Bliss. She asked me to go with her, but I declined." *I had to rob a bank to pay off Conrad.* "If I was there, she wouldn't have been in that alley, and she wouldn't have been attacked."

"Don't put this on yourself."

"I already have."

"The detective is going to want to know if she was meeting someone there, if she was dating anyone, any reason she might walk into a dark alley."

"I don't have those answers..." *But the detective might give me a clue as to what he knows...if he's zeroing in on Conrad or off on a wild goose chase...*

"Alright. I'll talk to him. What's his name?"

"Kellerman."

"Is he any good?"

"I know little about him. He's new to the force...from NYPD."

"I wonder if he knew my dad."

"Maybe, but I'm sure he'll be thorough."

"Yeah...we'll see about that." Jesse had to get to Conrad's place. "I gotta go."

As fate would have it, on a night of horror and miracles, the Corolla started.

Chapter Nine

The horizon was just cracking dawn as Jesse drove his rattletrap down a rutted and pothole-infested dirt road toward Conrad's trailer parked deep in the woods near a pond with no name. This morning's terror rode on his shoulder; the horrifying image of Clarissa was etched in his mind like chisel to stone. Conrad was the vicious maniac who'd bushwhacked her, the work of a true psychopath.

Hot rage seared through his veins at the thought of that piece of shit bookie. *"Pay up by tomorrow, or I'll visit your sister, and it won't be a cordial call."*

Gravel and dirt flew up from his tires as they skidded and jostled the Corolla along the rough road. The dust mixed with oily smoke in the car's wake. Conrad's day of reckoning was barreling down on him with a vengeance.

After another mile, he reached the clearing where a forty-foot mobile home rested on concrete blocks. Slabs of siding were missing from the exterior, and a dilapidated wood porch reached several steps up to the front entrance and its bent screen door. The smell of raw sewage tainted the early-morning air. Ragged and water-stained drapes were drawn shut, and vapor drifted up from a rooftop vent. His black gas-guzzling Ford truck looked out of place parked in front of this dump. Empty Budweiser cans and Jack Daniels bottles lay about a firepit in a weed-infested lawn. He'd probably be sleeping off a hangover 'til noon.

Jesse parked behind the truck, left the Corolla engine running to ensure a quick getaway, got out, and opened the trunk from which he removed the rope and the chainsaw. With his luck, he probably wouldn't find a descent enough chair to tie the bastard to. Getting him into that chair would be another problem unto itself. He grabbed the tire iron and wished he had a gun.

As he trekked toward the front door, he passed the truck and thought to touch the hood, expecting it to be at least warm, if not hot. However, to his chagrin, it was cold as a grave. It must've been parked there all night. If so, he couldn't have been Clarissa's attacker.

Shit.

That left him only one recourse. He had to speak with the detective on the case, Kellerman, from New

York City, and hope to get a better grip on what direction the investigation was headed.

Before he walked back to the Corolla, he considered vandalizing the truck, flattening the tires, at least, but decided against it. So far tonight, by some miracle, he had not yet committed a crime. It would be stupid to start with something so petty. He returned the rope, chainsaw, and tire iron to the trunk, got in behind the wheel, and made good his retreat.

***

Jesse returned to his apartment above the Hudson View Laundromat in town. The stairs creaked with every step upward, and there was barely enough light to see the keyhole in his paint-starved door. After he entered, he ignored the cracks in the whitish-yellow walls, and the water spots that splotched the ceiling. Since being evicted from his swank apartment, on unemployment, he could only afford this low-rent dump, but he kept it clean. He dropped his keys on the table and flopped onto the bed. After he cocooned himself in the blankets, he fell into a fitful sleep:

He battled fierce winds and battering rain to reach Clarissa in the hospital. His breath shuddered as she wheezed through a tube down her throat, and as he observed her mummy wrappings, she rose like a specter. With a pallid hand, she ripped the IV needle from her arm, and lumbering toward him, she raised her arms, zombie-like, and groaned. "Why didn't you go with me, Jesse?" Her voice was monotone and eerie, ghostly he feared. "To the Bliss, like I asked you?"

"I'm sorry, Clarissa. I didn't know..."

"Why aren't you doing more to find the man who did this to me? It's not Conrad. The killer is out there somewhere, sharpening his blade for another attack."

"The cops are working the case."

"What are you doing? Sleeping? That's all you can do? Sleep?"

"I've been up all night. I'm tired."

"And I'm dying. Can't you see?" She dragged all the beeping machines behind her, wheels rattling. An IV stand crashed to the floor. Glass shattered. Blood pumped through all the tubes, spurted and spilled, splattering all over the floor. "It's all your fault, Jesse."

Her beauty had morphed into a pale-faced, black-eyed corpse, and as she neared, her form changed into a huge dark figure brandishing a shiny blade as he approached with long strides.

Small Town Killer

Jesse tried to run, but his feet were leaden, and the floor was slippery with Carissa's blood. His every move was in slow motion. There was no escape.

"Don't be a bigger fool than you already are, Jesse. You'll never find out who I am, but I'll always be your worst nightmare. All you care about is yourself. You don't care about Clarissa. And robbing a bank? Are you that stupid?"

Jesse had no choice but to stand his ground. "You're not going to get away with this."

Clarissa's hospital bed appeared out of the gloom, spinning and circling around him while the machines and tubes and wires streamed behind. Clarissa lay prone, strapped to the bed, screaming, "Jesse, save me. Jesse, where are you?"

Dread filled his chest. "Look what you've done to her."

The dark figure flicked the blade and glided closer to him as if floating on air. "I'm coming for her to finish the job."

"Stay away from her."

"I'll cut her into small pieces, take my time 'til she begs me to slit her throat, put her out of her misery."

"Why? She's done nothing to you. Nothing."

"And you can do nothing to stop me, Jesse.

You're a nobody. A loser."

The blade sliced across his throat. He gagged.

A spray of red jarred him from the dream. He sat up straight, his hands clutching his throat. No knife. No blood. Just his apartment. Sweat soaked his face as his heart slammed against his ribs. "No, no, no," he screamed. "Clarissa..." he gasped..."I'm gonna find the son of bitch who did this to you." He balled his fists and broke down in tears. "I'm sorry I wasn't there with you," he sobbed out. "I had a bank to rob. I'm sorry. I'm sorry. I'm so sorry." He slugged his pillow over and over and bawled and bawled and bawled.

It took an eon for him to calm down. He realized he was hungry and that sunlight shined through the west window. *What time is it?* He groped for his phone on the nightstand, saw several missed calls from the Peekskill PD. *3:03 p.m.*

Shit.

He had to get to the police station, talk to the detective. Keith told him Kellerman wanted more information about Clarissa in hopes it'll help him solve the case...but was that the extent of it? Maybe he knew Jesse's car had been spotted near the bank. Maybe he wanted to know why... *Why am I so paranoid? I did nothing wrong,* well, except attempted bank robbery, maybe.

What evidence could the cops have that could convict him of planning a bank heist? Had he missed a camera somewhere? Was he on video, unloading the tools of a bank robber from the trunk? The prosecutor would have to prove intent. Possessing a chainsaw, ladder, and rope did not make him a bank robber beyond a reasonable doubt.

I was going to trim a tree.

What tree?

A Christmas Tree.

It's the middle of summer.

I meant firewood, cut firewood.

At two a o'clock in the morning?

I wanted to get an early start.

He'd be caught in a lie. A jury would surely convict him, find him guilty of planning the notorious Peekskill Bank Caper. Would the court show leniency for a first-time offender? With his luck, Sing Sing Prison doors would welcome him, but slam shut behind him, the clang echoing down the halls, reverberating in the cells of hardened criminals. Inmates would laugh when they learned of his botched bank robbery. Some would lay claim to him. Fresh meat. "That's my bitch. Don't touch him." "Nah, bro, I saw him first."

He'd been such an idiot, looking for a quick fix to solve his problem, appease Conrad so the thug wouldn't go on a leg-breaking rampage. Desperate times called for desperate measures. Still, by the end of the day, he could be confined to a wheelchair, legs in plaster casts up to his crotch, and he'd still owe Conrad ten grand.

Shit. Shit. Shit.

He checked the voicemail; Keith had called three times. "Where the hell are you? The detective was waiting, but he had to go out to follow a lead."

Damn, I'm screwed.

A fist pounded on his door. Terror gripped his throat. Conrad was here to collect...or maybe it was Keith, here to arrest him. *I'm not that lucky.* The pounding got louder. "I'm coming, goddamnit. Let me get my pants on."

Half dressed, he answered the door. It was Keith. "I know. I know. I'm late."

He walked in, took off his duty cap. "You look like shit, man."

"Bad night." He slipped into a shirt. "Hear anything about Clarissa's case?"

"Not yet. I was worried about you."

"Did you think I skipped town?" Jesse put on his shoes. "I have to talk to the detective."

"He'll be back at five."

"I hope I can help, but don't know how." He took inventory: shirt tucked in, belt belted, wallet, phone, keys... "And I need to get to the hospital to check on Clarissa."

"Relax, your mom and uncle flew in this morning. They're at the hospital now."

"That helps. I'll see you down at the station."

"Okay, but don't dally. Nobody wants to work late." He set on his duty cap, left the door open, and clambered down the rickety steps to the street.

A few minutes later, sitting in his junker, he considered his close call with the Apple Farm's security guard and felt fortunate not to have gotten far enough to get busted cutting a hole in the bank's roof. He decided to take the long way to the station via Home Depot to get rid of the evidence.

It took him ten minutes to get there. He commandeered a cart and wheeled the burglary equipment to the customer service counter. While he stood in the RETURNS line, he saw Al approaching, his eyes big around.

"Hey, soldier, you're back so soon? What's wrong with the chainsaw? It's not working? From my experience, those are very reliable."

"No. It's fine, I guess. I never tried it. The truth

is, I can't afford to buy all this stuff. Screw the neighbors."

"I get it. Your heart was in the right place. Hey, I'm here if you need any help."

"Are you guys hiring?"

Al frowned. "Sorry, kid. Try back in a couple months."

With Home Depot in the rearview mirror, he felt a little better having the cash in his shirt pocket. He turned into Dunkin' drive-thru to get a coffee. Even this late in the day, the line of cars was long. *Why not splurge a little?* "I'll have a Macchiato," he said into the kiosk.

"Six dollars at the first window."

He drove around the building and stopped at the line of cars idling alongside the alley, waiting for the first window. A cloud of blue smoke enveloped the Corolla, reminding him he'd have to check the oil.

A bang on the roof made him jump. The passenger door opened, and out of the smoke emerged Conrad's hulk. He got in and closed the door like he owned the car. "Where you been all day, Jesse?"

"Fuck. You scared the shit out of me, man."

"I'm still short ten grand."

"Come on, Conrad. I've got the same problem.

Sorry I can't help you."

The line moved forward. The blue smoke followed the Corolla.

"Sorry don't count for nothing, you piece of shit loser. People gonna come after me for their cut. What do I tell them, Jesse? Do I give them your name? They shoot to kill."

"Go ahead, break my legs if it'll make you feel better. You and your cronies still won't get any money."

"Can't give them your sister's name. I hear somebody already got to her. Who else do you owe?"

"Why does it have to be my fault?"

"Everything is your fault, loser."

"Shit, Conrad. Haven't you heard that patience is a virtue?"

"I have no virtues."

"I'll get you your money as soon as I can."

He glared at Jesse, jaw moving from side to side then clenched his fist. "That's not good enough."

"Get out of my car."

Conrad slugged him with a brutal punch to the side of his head. Fiery pain shot through his skull, and his vision flashed on and off. The car rocked on its springs. Conrad yanked him across the console and went nose-to-nose with him. "Don't fuck with me."

"What the hell, man?" Jesse gasped for air.

"I should kill you right here, but there are too many witnesses." His tobacco breath was as lethal as venom. He patted Jesse's pockets. "What's this? You've been holding out on me?" He removed the folded cash from Jesse's shirt pocket and shoved him back into the seat. "You got anything else?"

Jesse rubbed the side of his head. "That's all I got to my name, man. Please—"

A horn honked behind him. The line had moved forward two car lengths.

Conrad peeled a ten from the wad and dropped it on the console. "Coffee's on me, fool. You better come up with the rest by tomorrow." He opened the door and vanished in the blue smoke.

***

In the ICU ward at Hudson Valley Hospital, Jude sat slumped next to her daughter. Strands of blond hair peeked out through gaps in the bandages that wrapped around her head and face. A breathing tube protruded from a slit in the white tape over her mouth. The whispering rhythmic beeping and rasping of life-support machines chilled the heart of a mother in deep despair. She squeezed Clarissa's bandaged hand. "My poor baby."

Bright purple balloons tethered to the bed hovered above, their joyous faces smiling down. A yellow and red banner on the wall read: GET WELL SOON. WE LOVE YOU, CLARISSA. Crystal vases held a splay of red roses, and beams of sunlight streamed in through the skylight and landed on her bed like arriving angels.

Uncle Francis stood beside Jude, his graying hair cropped short and his belly protruding, a monument to his success, he'd boasted. That and his sporty clothes: white polo, brown slacks, and Nike golf shoes spoke of his prowess on the fairway as a pro golfer. He rested his hand on her shoulder. "Hang in there, sis. Think positive. She's going to get better."

"Francis, look at her, all the bandages...God has forsaken us."

"God had nothing to do with what happened to her."

"I pray to him every day...to protect my children..." She sobbed and clutched her gold-cross necklace with trembling fingers. "And look what he's allowed to happen."

"Jude, I'm sorry for what the devil has done, and you're right, she doesn't look good, but I believe God is watching over her...else she'd be dead by now."

"Why would anyone do this to her? It's

senseless."

"The doctors are doing everything they can. The coma will give her a fighting chance to heal."

Jude gasped as she witnessed an amorphous shape, an aura floating above Clarissa's body and rising in the sunbeam, out through the skylight, and ascending toward the heavens. She fell to her knees and clapped her hands together in prayer.

Francis's eyes widened. "What is it, Jude?"

"I saw my daughter's soul going up to Heaven."

"You and your visions. Get hold of yourself, Jude." He pointed to the blipping heart machine. "She's alive. Look at the monitors."

Clarissa shuddered.

Jude shot to her feet and gripped her daughter's bandaged hand again. Hope blossomed in her heart. "She's waking up. Dear God, it's a miracle."

"There's no way—"

"Get the nurse. My baby's coming back to me. Clarissa. Clarissa," she screamed.

A nurse rushed in. "What's going on?"

"She's waking up."

The nurse frowned, checked the machines, and shook her head. "There's no change."

"But she moved."

"It's not abnormal for someone in a coma to

move a little. I've even seen them open their eyes, but their stares are blank."

"So...she's not waking up?"

"I'm sorry."

Jude's mouth dropped.

"I must go." The nurse backstepped to the gap in the curtain. "But don't worry. I'll keep an eye on her." She left.

Jude blinked away tears. "I shouldn't have gone to Florida. This can't be happening. Call Jesse...he should be here by now."

"I'm sure he's on his way." He put his hands on her shoulders and pulled her into a comforting hug. "We're here. That's what matters now."

Jude sobbed.

Chapter Ten

Kellerman arrived at the hospital and displayed his credentials to a nurse with short brown hair and taut arms. The smell of disinfectant lingered in the air. "I'm here to see Clarissa Curley."

Lines of worry wrinkled her brow. "She's in ICU. Third floor. You look like you could use a cup of coffee. Rough day?"

"You could say that, but I'm good. How's Miss Curley doing?"

"I don't know. You'll have to ask the duty nurse." She gestured toward the elevators.

On the third floor, he stepped out of the elevator into a hallway that led to double doors marked ICU. He approached the nurses station on the right. Must've been a dozen medical personnel behind the counter, all busy at monitors or conversing in the background. He cleared his throat and waved his badge.

"May I help you?"

"Clarissa Curley. Where is she?"

"She's in a coma. You can't talk to her."

"I'm investigating the assault, need to see how bad a shape she's in...for the record."

"Bed number two." She pressed a button on the counter.

"I'll go with him," another nurse said. She wore scrubs and a net over her red hair.

The double doors opened.

He followed the redhead to an opening in curtain number two. A man and woman stood at the patient's bedside. "Her parents?"

"Mother and uncle. Flew in from Florida, been here since noon, brought the balloons and banner, as if they would do any good. That poor girl. It's horrible what happened."

"Yeah, horrible."

She clenched her fists. "Please catch the animal that did this to her. Shoot him in the head. He doesn't deserve a trial."

"I'll keep that in mind, ma'am."

"I've got to get back to my post."

"Sure." As her footsteps receded, he lingered at the curtain, hoping to hear something that might hint at how close she was to death.

"I hope they catch whoever did this," the mother said.

"Maybe it was someone she was dating."

"I doubt it. Clarissa is so independent..." She hesitated to wipe her nose with a tissue. "I was waiting for the day she brought someone home. Someone she loved, but that day never came."

Kellerman took note: *No boyfriend.*

"The early twenties are confusing times," the uncle said. "Kids think they're adults but lack maturity. Experience is the teacher. Somehow she hadn't learned that dark alleys are dangerous."

"Clarissa is a good kid. Smart. She wouldn't do anything stupid. Whatever it was, she had good reason to go back there."

"Maybe she got in with the wrong crowd... went behind the club to get a fix—"

"Stop. Don't even say that."

"I'm just saying...she might have picked up some bad habits in college. Wouldn't be the first time."

"Not a chance. She'd never do drugs. I know my daughter, and we talked most every day."

Kellerman took note: *No drug addiction.*

The nurse returned. "You okay, detective?"

"Oh, yes."

Mother and Uncle turned, eyes wide with surprise.

"Just checking my notes." He entered and approached the startled pair. "Excuse me. I'm sorry to intrude. I'm Detective Kellerman with the Peekskill PD. This is my case."

The mother glared at him. "What are you doing here? Shouldn't you be out there looking for the bastard responsible for this...this horror."

"Jude, please," the uncle said. "Take it easy."

She swallowed and sobbed. Tears streamed from her red and puffy eyes. "Look at what he did to my baby."

"That's why I'm here, ma'am."

Worry mottled the uncle's face, his eyes bloodshot for lack of rest. "I'm Francis McMahon...my sister here, Jude Curley, please forgive her outbursts."

This ordeal is hell on earth for them. "I fully understand." Kellerman focused on the victim, catatonic and connected to life-sustaining machines. The knife had punched her full of holes...should've killed her. "The world is full of crazy and unfortunate circumstances." He returned his gaze to the mother and uncle. "I don't know how she survived."

"She's a tough girl, detective." Jude wiped tears off her face with her sleeve. "How close are you to finding him?"

He knew his answer would sound bad, but it was necessary to draw out a legitimate line of questioning. "I've got nothing so far. Maybe you can help. How close were you to your daughter...before this?"

Jude narrowed her eyes. "What is that supposed to mean?"

"Maybe she confided in you about someone she was uncomfortable with, a stalker maybe, or a guy bothering her."

"She hangs with the wrong crowd, I can tell you that. Clubbers they're called. Out all night. No fear of the streets. Bet she'll listen to her mother after this...if she gets better." The tears flowed again.

"Where else does she hang out besides the Bliss?" Another legit question.

"She likes dive bars for the vibe of the working class, she'd said. No telling what riffraff she'd crossed paths with there."

"Glitz to grunge, huh?"

"That's my Clarissa. She respects everyone, no matter their lot in life."

"When did you last talk to her?"

Jude glanced at Francis. "A week ago. Before we left for Florida."

"Did she seem normal or agitated?"

"Clarissa? Agitated? Not this party girl. She didn't want to go on vacation with us...just had to stay here and enjoy her freedom after graduating from college. If she'd have come with us, she'd be happy and fancy-free today...instead of in this mess." More tears.

Francis put his arm around her shoulder.

Kellerman rubbed the two-day stubble on his chin. Everyone hoped she'd recover, except the attacker, and he wondered if she might have seen just enough to identify him. "Can you think of anything she wasn't happy about...worried about? Anything, even if you think it's insignificant...anything might help me solve this case."

"She's an angel, a perfect person in a cruel world. Her biggest mistake was not seeing the world for what it truly is." Jude crossed her heart. "There's a maniac out there, detective. I wish I could help you find him, but you're on your own."

"Yeah." Working in law enforcement exposed him to parts of society most people didn't want to see or even know about. Just handle the criminals; that's all society wanted from him. He'd seen the worst of the worst, the dregs of the human race, especially in New York City, where gangs shot at each other and innocent children got caught in the crossfire.

That tragedy didn't seem all that long ago, when the neighborhood basketball court shootout changed his life forever. He remembered gripping the wheel of his squad car, knuckles turning white, as he sped to the hospital. The emergency room was chaos, gang members and cops lying about, bleeding and moaning, but he was looking for a little girl, his daughter Deirdre, an innocent victim of the war for home turf and gang supremacy. He found her in a children's ward, a small body hooked up to big machines, where a doctor gave him the bad news.

"The bullet severed her spinal cord at C5. She almost bled out before anyone got to her. Meanwhile, she couldn't breathe on her own, and the lack of oxygen to her brain caused severe and irreparable damage."

It was hard being a cop in New York City, but this tragedy turned worse when the ballistics report came in. The bullet came from an officer's service weapon. *Most likely a ricochet, judging from the deformation of the projectile.* It was ruled a terrible accident in the heat of battle. One of his own, a brother in blue, had destroyed his daughter's life, her future, and tore his family apart.

After his wife's suicide, Kellerman relocated to Peekskill, a small town on a bend in the Hudson River, a peaceful place, until now. He remembered transferring his daughter to Hudson Valley Children's Sanctum so he could be closer to her, leveraging connections to orchestrate a transfer that coincided with his official retirement from NYPD. To maintain her anonymity, he'd checked her in as Deirdre Dodson.

He felt a hand squeeze his arm. "Detective, are you okay?" Jude asked him.

He blinked back to the moment and took a deep breath. "Sorry. This kind of crime never gets easier to accept."

She removed her hand. "You must have seen a lot."

"You could say that." He checked the time. Going on 5 p.m. "I have to get back to the station to interrogate a suspect." He handed her a card. "Let me know if anything comes to mind...if anything changes."

Back in his Tahoe, he exhaled a long breath. *Now to see what Jesse Curley has to say for himself.*

***

Nursing a lump on his head and a coffee he could no longer afford, Jesse drove to the police station on Nelson Ave and pulled into the public parking garage across the street from the brick CITY OF PEEKSKILL POLICE building. After he parked, he left the coffee in the cup holder to get cold and crossed over to the steps leading down to the front door. Standing between two anti-vehicle intrusion posts, painted blue, he looked up to the second floor, where narrow barred windows looked down on him like the weeping eyes of an old man. Probably the city jail where he hoped he wouldn't end up, dressed in black and white stripes and guarding his backside. He felt fortunate his bank robbery plan had fallen short.

Inside, a sergeant handled the duty desk. His uniform shirt looked stretched to the limit across his broad shoulders, and his head was tilted down, revealing a bald spot in the middle of his wiry gray hair. He didn't even show the common courtesy of looking up from a paperback he held in front of him.

"I'm here to see detective Kellerman."

He pointed toward a doorway marked SECURITY.

"Thanks." There Jesse found himself in a hall blocked by a walk-through metal detector. An officer waved him forward.

"Got any weapons on you?"

"No, sir." When he passed through, the machine emitted a frantic beeping sound.

"Hold up there," the cop said.

"Must be my keys."

The cop held out a plastic tray. "Empty your pockets."

Jesse took out his car keys, the change left over from the coffee purchase, and his barren wallet, dropped it all in the tray.

"And your belt."

"My belt?"

"And take off your shoes."

"What? Why?" Jesse's pulse surged.

"Haven't you been through airport security before?"

"This is a police station."

"You look nervous...like you're guilty of something...can't be too careful."

Shoes and belt off, and holding his pants up so they wouldn't slip down to his ankles, he walked through the detector again, this time with no complaint from the machine.

"See?" the cop handed him the tray. "That wasn't so hard, was it?"

"Says the guy who hasn't been humiliated for no good reason." After putting himself back together, he proceeded to a waiting area: vinyl chairs, vending machines, magazine rack, where he claimed a chair opposite an elderly woman who sat with her arms crossed over a purse on her lap. He hoped his blood pressure and his breathing would settle soon.

A heavy-set man wearing a Rent-A-Cop jacket

plodded into the waiting area and took a seat two chairs from him. "What are you in for?" He laughed at his own joke. "I'm here to see Detective Morrison."

That voice. He'd heard that gruff voice before. *Hey. You can't sleep here. This car better be gone when I come around again or I'll have it towed. Piece of junk.*

Oh, great. Stay cool. "Detective Kellerman."

"The new homicide dick. Who did you kill?" Another belly laugh followed.

"Funny man. My sister was attacked. What are you doing here?"

"Morrison in Robbery needs this." He pulled a sheathed disc from his inside pocket. "Video surveillance from Apple Farm Commons. I thwarted a bank heist."

"Good for you." *Shit. He's got the security footage from the bank. Somehow I missed a camera...*but still, there couldn't possibly be any evidence of a bank robbery in progress. Besides, the cameras weren't operating properly, needed a software upgrade, so anything on that disc would be grainy, at best.

"You okay, buddy?" The guard asked him. "You're looking a little pale."

"Worried about my sister, is all."

The guard's eyes narrowed. "You look familiar to me. Have we met somewhere before?"

Jesse's pulse shot up again. He was right. They'd made eye contact as he passed by on his second time around. *Just as I was leaving...* He shrugged. "I think I'd have remembered you...but I don't."

"Yeah...maybe not, but—"

A door swung open, and footsteps approached. Jesse whirled to find a tall man dressed in a suit striding forward. Maybe the detective. The man glanced at him then addressed the guard. "Mr. Simpson. Good of you to come in."

The guard stood. "Detective Morrison. Always a pleasure."

"I see you brought the video."

The guard waggled the disc. "It's all here."

"Come on back to my office."

As they pushed through a door to the squad rooms, another man entered, a linebacker in a suit with a gold police badge clipped on his belt. "Mr. Curley?"

Jesse stood. "You must be Detective Kellerman."

The detective's forehead had ripples etched into it. Darkened skin drooped under his eyes. Overworked. Overstressed, Jesse assumed. Reminded him of his dad...before he was gunned down while on patrol in New York City.

"Let's make this quick. I'm sure you have better

things to do than hang around here all night."

#

Kellerman directed Jesse toward an interview room, aka *the box*. He passed the vacant break room with a fridge, microwave, toaster oven, and caught the lingering scent of coffee.

Detectives utilized *the box* for initial questioning, to gather information from witnesses, nothing official. Suspect interrogations took place in a more secure room, *the cage,* which was heavily monitored and recorded. If a suspect's body language made him or her look guilty, he'd make them feel comfortable. Let them talk, catch them in a lie and tighten their own nooses. This method worked on most suspects, but some hated the police and showed no respect. "You're wasting your time, pig," or "I know my rights," or "You ain't got shit on me." Those were the tough nuts Kellerman loved to crack.

Once seated at a small table in a small room, he sized up Jesse Curley. His body language shouted frazzled nerves. He had to be guilty of something. It might be *the cage* for him next.

***

Detective Morrison led the bulky security guard to his cubicle in Robbery, Burglary, and Petty Larceny. He wouldn't have any problem getting information from a wannabe police officer who couldn't make the big leagues.

Seated, Morrison went to work. "For the record, this meeting is being recorded. I've got a report here from Officer Keith Clarkson." He tapped a file on top of a pile on his desk. "The primary on a call to your patrol area. You told him what you saw, and you claim to have video of a bank robbery in progress."

"Right here, detective." He handed the disc to Morrison, who set it on top of the file.

"Aren't you going to look at it?"

"Later." He leaned back in his chair. "Tell me about the car."

"Old Toyota Corolla. It's all on the video."

"Can you ID the driver?"

"Thirty, maybe, average looking."

Morrison grumped. "That could be anybody."

"It was dark, but I saw him."

"Does this video show him breaking into the bank?"

"Well, no...but he had a ladder, a chainsaw, and a rope."

"Is that on this video?"

"No, but just as I turned the corner, I saw him stash the stuff into his trunk. And he took off a ski mask, and I swear he answered a phone call then jumped into the back seat. Real suspicious, if you ask me...in fact, now that I think about it, I'm pretty sure the guy is sitting in your waiting room."

"For real?"

"I thought I'd seen him somewhere before."

"Hang tight while I check it out." Morrison headed for the waiting area.

***

Feeling uneasy about being scrutinized, Jesse stared at Kellerman. "You're looking at me like I'm some kind of criminal."

"I have that way with people."

"I just want to know what you've learned about my sister's attacker. How close are you to solving the case?"

"I'm the one who asks the questions around here."

Jesse pressed further. "Do you have any suspects?"

"Not yet, but—"

"Then why are you wasting your time with me? You should be out there pounding the streets—"

Kellerman shot up from his chair and stabbed a finger at him. "You don't tell me how to run an investigation. I'm in charge. Not you."

Jesse leaned back. "What can I do to help?"

"Tell me what you and your sister know about your dad's murder."

"My dad? What's he got to do with this?"

"I did my research." Kellerman stepped closer. "You think I don't get the connection here? Seamus Curley, shot dead in the city, Clarissa Curley, knifed in an alley, and you, Jesse Curley, as yet unharmed."

Jesse felt his face flush. "You think I'm next?"

"I think you should watch your back."

"Why? What's this all about?"

"A bullet from your dad's gun paralyzed a nine-year-old girl. Do you think somebody might want revenge for that?"

"It was an accident—"

A knock on the door interrupted him.

"What is it?" Kellerman shouted.

The door opened, and that Morrison detective guy stepped in. "I'm going to need to see your boy there," he tilted his head to Jesse, "when you're done."

Jesse's heart lurched. "Me?"

Kellerman scowled. "What for?"

"Oh, not much. Just a little attempted bank robbery."

Now Jesse jumped up. "What did that slimy security guard tell you? I didn't do anything wrong."

Jim Keane

"I've got video and eye witness testimony." Morrison frowned. "I'd like to hear what you have to say."

"Come on. That guard is looking for fifteen minutes of fame."

Kellerman stepped between them, facing Jesse. "One more stupid comment out of you, I'll arrest you myself."

Jesse opened his mouth to say they were both crazy, but he figured he'd pushed them far enough. Besides, he didn't have an endgame, and he was no good to Clarissa in jail.

Kellerman clenched his jaw, then: "Consider your next words wisely, Mr. Curley."

"Do I need a lawyer?" *Who am I kidding? I can't afford a lawyer.*

Morrison shrugged. "I don't know. Do you?"

Kellerman turned to Morrison. "You'll have to wait. I've got him first."

"I'll be in my office." Morrison closed the door.

Kellerman pointed to the chair. "Sit down."

"I know my rights."

"They all do. Sit."

Steamed, Jesse sat. "He's got nothing on me."

Kellerman reclaimed his chair. "You having money problems?"

"Don't we all?"

"Attempted bank robbery is serious shit, son."

"What do you care? You're homicide."

"Major Crimes. Homicide. Take your pick. Do you have a girlfriend?"

"What's it to you?"

"Somebody has to care about you. You sure don't."

Jesse mulled it over. He had dated several women, but nothing serious. College was one party after another, but no enduring relationships blossomed. With no work and a recent eviction, he worried more about his economic situation than his love situation, or lack thereof. Sure, he'd settle down if he found the right woman, but right now he wasn't a good catch...with no job, no prospects, and no decent place to live. So the answer was simple. "No. No girlfriend."

Kellerman rolled his eyes. "Come on. A good-looking guy like you." Sarcasm laced his words. "A line of beauties must be at your door."

"You haven't seen my door." Jesse shook his head, irritated by the taunts. *What does this cop have against me?*

"I'm a Curley. Is that what this is all about?"

"You tell me."

"How should I know? My dad was a good cop. Had a run of bad luck, is all. I'm sorry about the girl. She was in the wrong place at the wrong time."

"She was on a basketball court where she belonged, where she thrived. NYPD had no business confronting that gang while she was in harm's way."

"I had nothing to do with that."

"Your dad did, and he ended up dead. Maybe he deserved to die."

Jesse leaped up, fists balled. "You can't say that about my dad. Take it back. He'd do anything for anybody."

Kellerman shoved Jesse against the wall, face first. "You're under arrest."

"For what?"

"Assaulting a police officer."

"I didn't touch you."

"Hands behind your back."

The cuffs clicked on around his wrists, tightly, of course.

"You have the right to remain silent. I suggest you do just that."

"I need to see Clarissa."

"Anything you say may be used against you in a court of law."

"This is wrong."

"You have a right to an attorney. If you can't afford an attorney, the court will appoint one for you."

"Is that supposed to be a plus, you asshole?"

"Do you understand these rights?"

"Let me go."

Kellerman pushed him back into the chair. "You're not going anywhere." He stormed out and slammed the door.

"Goddamnit. You can't do this to me."

Chapter Eleven

While Jesse slouched on a hard mattress in the city jail, his face buried in his hands and his mind consumed by frustration and worry, a clang of metal and thudding footfalls echoed from down the corridor. *Probably one of Kellerman's other victims of police brutality.*

The footsteps stopped at his cell door. "Look what you've gone and done now, Jess."

He looked up to see Keith standing there, arms folded across his chest, all cop-righteous. Jesse groaned. "Kellerman's got it out for me."

"Assault on a police officer? What's the matter with you?"

"I never touched him." He stood and stepped to the bars. "Where's Kellerman?"

"Investigating Clarissa's case...at the Bliss."

"That guy is an asshole. You should have heard the shit he said about my dad."

"No mention of your dad in the arrest affidavit, just the assault and how you resisted arrest."

"No way. The interrogation room video will

prove I'm innocent." He hesitated to swallow a lump in his throat. "They all have video, right?"

"Sorry, Jess, not in *the box*, and no one was available to monitor the conversation. Skeleton crew after 5 p.m., and Detective Doherty is out on vacation. Still, as I cop, I wonder about motivation. Why would he have a burr up his butt for you?"

"He told me flat out. Some little girl got shot in a New York City gang bust, and he's taken it personally."

"It's hard not to get emotionally invested in a crime. You could say it's a hazard of the job."

"He blames my dad, and he's not upset about his murder, thinks the attack on Clarissa might be connected, warned me to watch my back, and then he did this to me." He waved a hand to the confines of his cell. "Any updates on her condition?"

Keith glanced down. "No change."

Jesse grabbed the bars. "You've got to get me out of here."

"It'll take time. You'll need a public defender." Keith rubbed his chin. "I think I know just the guy."

"I can't afford a lawyer."

"The state will cover the tab."

"I hope he's got room for two cases on his schedule."

Jim Keane

"Two? What are you talking about?"

"You told Detective Morrison where I was Friday night."

"I'm required to submit a report on every complaint I investigate. Nothing personal."

"That damn security guard is a glory hound, wants credit for thwarting a crime that never happened. Morrison's going to charge me with attempted bank robbery."

Keith peered around and back at Jesse. "If you were there to rob the bank, it's better to admit it now."

"Really?" Jesse's face burned with anger. "I can't believe you said that. How long have we been friends?"

"Doesn't matter. Nobody is above the law. You put yourself in a bad situation, Jess."

"The security guard brought video evidence, so he says, but I didn't do anything illegal."

"Goes to intent. Be honest. What were you doing there, a long way from your apartment, at two o'clock in the morning?"

"Just because I was there doesn't mean I've turned to a life of crime."

He huffed. "And look at you now, behind bars...just like a criminal. What you say and what I see are two different things, Jess."

"Just get me a lawyer. Maybe he'll have my back."

"We'll see what tomorrow brings."

"Tomorrow? What happens then?"

"You'll see a judge for a bail hearing. If you can't pay it, you'll have to stay in here until the arraignment and trial."

"They can't keep me locked up in here on a bogus charge."

"Sure they can."

Jesse collapsed back onto the mattress and buried his face in his hands while footfalls receded and steel doors clanged.

***

It was 10 p.m. when Kellerman arrived at the Bliss Nightclub. The music was loud, the patrons rowdy, and the dance floor was packed. Strobe lights caused him a bit of vertigo as he pressed through the crowd to the bar, his badge leading the way. "I'm here to see the owner, Nick Fortune." He had to yell over all the noise.

"Over there." He pointed down the bar with a Jameson bottle in his hand. "The guy wearing the fedora."

Kellerman strode past occupied bar stools to the

owner. He looked to be about fifty, gray goatee, sharp dresser, gold paisley vest over a white button-down, brown hat worn low over his brow. He sipped clear liquid from a short tumbler, maybe a vodka tonic on ice. Kellerman cleared the adjacent stool with the flash of his badge to its lanky occupant and sat beside the owner. "Busy night," he shouted.

"Everybody's come to see where the girl got stabbed. Who would've thought blood and gore would be good for business?"

"That's why I'm here. Kellerman, Peekskill PD."

The owner slammed the remainder of his drink. "Fortune, Nick Fortune." After a quick handshake, he wiped his hand on his pant leg like a germophobe might do. "Glad to be of assistance."

"I hear you've got video of the alley."

"I do...in my office downstairs." When he stood from the barstool, the butt of a gun in his waistband became clearly visible.

Kellerman stood as well. "I see you're packing."

"Never leave home without it." Fortune turned and patted the gun. "I—"

"Don't reach." Kellerman set his hand close to the slat in his jacket, to be near his shoulder-harnessed Glock, in case things turned dicey.

"Oh, sorry." Fortune raised his hand. "I'm just

exercising my Second Amendment rights. I fought in the Middle East."

"Take it out. Two fingers. Slowly."

"I've got a CC, nice and legal like."

"Do it anyway."

Fortune carefully removed the gun, discreetly as to not panic nearby patrons.

Kellerman recognized it, a popular civilian weapon, a Smith and Wesson M&P 2.0 Series cannon. He took the gun, ejected the clip, cleared the chamber, and returned it to Fortune. "I'll hold the clip for you."

"I understand you can't be too careful, but I'm not the bad guy here."

"I don't know that...least not well enough to bet my life on it."

"In these times, it's essential to stay vigilant. I never know what will happen."

"The video. Let's go."

Fortune led him behind the bar and down a brightly lit stairwell to the basement. Aglow under fluorescent lights, computer monitors were lined up on a long table. Beer cases and kegs were stacked in an immense cooler, and boxes of wine and booze were stored against the near wall. Along the far wall, hay bales were stacked to the ceiling, a puzzling sight.

The row of monitors remained dormant until

Fortune clapped his hands. They powered up and a countdown appeared on the center screen, starting at thirty in bold Ariel fonts. He sat in a swivel chair. "Activate."

The numbers stopped counting down, and the desktop icons appeared.

"Voice activated," Kellerman stated, somewhat impressed at Fortune's security measures.

"The computer only responds to my voice." Fortune indicated another chair. "You can sit here."

He sat and rolled the chair closer to Fortune's screen. "Have you seen the video?"

"Not yet. I blocked off the time frame for Friday night."

"Can you make me a copy?"

"Of course. I can put it on a flash drive."

"That's fine. Let's see what you've got."

He clicked the play symbol.

The video started at 9 p.m. Partying patrons filled the dance floor.

"It'll be too hard to find her in this mass of idiocy. Can you switch to the front door to begin with patrons entering the bar? Once we spot her, we can follow her."

"Right here."

Partiers filed in, some en masse, some loners. IDs

passed back and forth. Jocularity seemed to abound though there was no audio.

"Can you speed it up?"

At four-X, the procession went by in a jerky whirl. When 11:20 rolled up on the digital clock, he spotted her in line.

"There."

Fortune clicked normal speed.

She showed her ID to the bouncer...

My God. So full of life. And pretty too, dressed to the nines in a loose black mini that showed lots of thigh, a red blouse that showed a hint of cleavage, high heels...not a care in the world as she strode to the bar, hugging and kissing friends she'd passed by.

She could have been his daughter, a pretty woman with lots of friends, a queen in her own right, her whole life ahead of her, *but fuck no.* A stray bullet from a cop's gun ended all of it. The more he watched Clarissa strut about, the more the heartache boiled into anger. Now Clarissa and his daughter were both breathing through tubes forced down their throats.

There was no justice in this world but the justice he dished out.

She met a guy, some macho type, a muscle-bound meathead in tight pants and a sleeveless shirt. *What the hell is she doing?* She fell into his arms, lavished him with hugs and kisses, like a common whore... *and look at that.* She was dirty-dancing with him on the dance floor...in front of everyone, rubbing backsides and copping feels... *My God...my daughter would never act like this.* As he watched the debauchery, the hairs on the nape of his neck jittered. The dancing went on forever, it seemed, but then a clue emerged as she and the dickhead moved hand-in-hand to the front door. Fortune switched views to show them standing under the marquee, and sure enough, they stepped out of camera range.

He made a mental note to find this guy and interview him, though he didn't think the knuckle-dragger saw anything that would be conclusive.

Fortune clicked the link to the alley-cam, and Kellerman saw the couple stop at the dumpster and gaze up at the sky like star-struck lovebirds. Then she sprinted, somewhat clumsily in those high heels, out through the perimeter of the alley light. Muscle-brains was not far behind.

It wasn't but a couple minutes later that a truck pulled into the alley and stopped. The two emerged from the surrounding darkness, both looking a bit disheveled. A man got out of the truck, slapped the kid upside the head, pointed to the girl, obviously reprimanding her by the scowl on his face, then the two males got into the truck and drove off.

The dumbasses left her alone in the alley.

She tidied herself up then she got the shock of her life. The look of fear on her face, even in the dim light, was palatable, almost delicious, if he were a connoisseur. Sure enough, there he was in all his bulk and glory, the knife clutched in his fist, striding toward his victim.

He focused on the masked face. The balaclava revealed only his eyes, and in such dim light, he couldn't make out the color.

"That could be anyone's face under the mask. Pause it and zoom in on the eyes."

The resultant close-up didn't reveal a clearer image.

Fortune resumed the video at regular speed and watched Clarissa put up one hell of a fight, even ran out of her shoes, managed to cut him with a jagged bottle neck, but he finally got her down and went to work on the kill, which turned his stomach to watch the brutality play out, until she collapsed motionless under his weight. He raised the blade for the coup-de-grâce when the cabbie came into view.

The attacker froze, and Kellerman could imagine what he was thinking. *Kill them both now or finish her off later.* He chose the latter and abandoned the attack.

Fortune stopped the video. "Did you see anything helpful?"

"I'll have to study it further at the precinct."

"I noticed one thing, detective, now I'm not saying it's you, but that guy sure is as big as you. Kinda walks like you, too, when I saw you walking toward me at the bar."

"Jeez. You're no help, man."

"You didn't notice that resemblance? I thought you cops noticed everything."

"I know I'd hate to go up against that guy, that's for sure. Make me a copy."

"Of the assault?"

"All of it."

"That's a lot of gigs, detective. It'll take a few hours to copy *all* the files. I'll send a flash drive over to the station tomorrow."

"You do that." Kellerman stood. "And keep your wise-guy mouth shut, you hear?"

"Look. My club has a good reputation, and all those people upstairs are here for the wrong reason. I want this guy caught as much as you do. Then things can get back to normal."

"Life will never be normal again. Get used to it."

"How's the girl?"

"She's not dead yet, if that's what you mean."

"I'll send her flowers."

"If I were you, I'd hire the best lawyers in town."

"What for?"

"Isn't it obvious? You can't keep your patrons safe. You can bet that girl's family will sue you down to your underwear."

"I need this business. It's my life."

"You should improve security."

"I'll hire more bouncers."

"That's a start."

Kellerman stormed out of the club with an uneasy feeling about Fortune and his *'looks like you'* bullshit.

***

Time was approaching the graveyard shift at the 24-Hour Peekskill Hometown Diner when Kellerman slumped into a worn booth. A server, somewhere in her fifties, scribbled down orders from patrons. Cutlery clinked and clattered, and the aroma of grilled onions hung deliciously in the air. He hunched over his cell phone, scrolling through pictures of Deirdre shooting hoops at the neighborhood basketball court. The memory of her perfect form, sinking jump shots with ease, filled his soul with pride. God, what promise the girl possessed.

"What's your poison, stranger?"

He looked up. The waitress had made it to his table, coffee pot at the ready.

"I'll take some of that coffee with a cheeseburger deluxe on the side, and double up on those onion rings."

"You must be hungry." She poured him a cup of brew. "New in town or just passing through?"

"New in town," he replied flatly.

"Oh, the pleasant type, I see."

"I'm not in the mood for chitchat. Just hungry, and I got a lot on my mind." After a last glance at Deirdre, he set the phone down. "And I haven't slept since that gal was stabbed behind the Bliss."

"Clarissa Curley. I heard. How awful. You a cop?"

"What did I say about chitchat?"

She shrugged. "Okay, I'll leave you to it."

He wasn't lying about having a lot on his mind. *That goddamned Nick Fortune had a lot of nerve saying I looked like the assailant.* Something fishy about that guy. All that security and a girl gets stabbed right under his nose. Not so smart, after all.

He sipped coffee, wondering what to do about Fortune. If he got to blabbing about his take on the video, it might muddle the investigation...*or was he deflecting suspicion away from himself and onto me?* That would be a classic move. And all those new patrons...the bar was packed. He had a lot to gain by setting up an attack on his premises. The DA might buy that theory. He'd need to turn the investigation toward Mr. Nick Fortune.

I better pay him a visit, this time on the record.

"Here you go, honey. Solved the world's problems yet?"

"Still working on it." He pulled the plate toward him.

"Enjoy." She hustled away.

He devoured the cheeseburger and munched on the onion rings. Mindless eating distracted him from the wreck that had become of his daughter. He'd visit her soon, despite the heartbreak of her condition.

He ran a hand over the stubble on his face. It wasn't a lie when he told the waitress he hadn't slept since the stabbing case was laid in his lap. Detective Doherty should've gotten it, he had seniority around here, but he lucked out, being on vacation, and all. In this line of work, sleep was a luxury. The Captain wanted the case solved ASAP. *Nothing like working under pressure.* However, staying busy helped keep his mind off his daughter.

"Anything else, darling?" the server asked while clearing the table.

Jim Keane

"The burger tasted like a hockey puck."

She indicated the empty plates. "You ate the whole thing. It couldn't have been that bad."

"Honestly, I've had worse...a lot worse."

"I'm happy to hear that."

He looked her up and down, noting the tousled hair and junk in the trunk. She wasn't terrible. "When do you get off work?"

Her cheeks reddened as she ripped a check from her pad and dropped it on the table. "When my husband picks me up."

"Never hurts to ask."

"You just made my night, baby. Thanks." She sauntered off with a little gimp in her step.

Women. Can't live with 'em, can't kill 'em.

Chapter Twelve

The next morning, an inmate, probably a trustee, delivered breakfast to Jesse's cell, slid the tray through a slit in the bars, just like in the movies. Cornflakes, a carton of sugar-sweetened milk, and a piece of bread that looked like it might have been toasted, dry and hard as a slab of slate. Better than nothing, but barely.

He hadn't slept a wink, it seemed, the noisy riffraff and heavy traffic snorted and clanged all night. And all the yelling...what the hell was that all about? As he'd lain there contemplating a bleak future, he couldn't stem the worry for Clarissa, the impending charges for assaulting that prick Kellerman, and worrying that Conrad was going to get his due in blood and broken bones. The throbbing knot on his head was testament to that. Top of the list, he had to quit gambling. Like his sister had said, *you're not very good at it.*

Not long after breakfast, Keith walked in, escorting a young man. He appeared to be fresh out of college, a regular frat boy with unkempt red hair and specks of stubble on his chin. Probably couldn't grow a beard if he pasted his face with testosterone and fertilizer. He wore a grey suit over an unbuttoned shirt with a striped tie loose at the knot.

Keith patted the guy on the back. "Jesse. This is Paul Garfield, your court-appointed attorney." Theatrically, Keith shook Paul's hand. "Thanks for coming on the show, Paul."

"No problem, Keith." Garfield turned to Jesse. "And you must be my client."

Jesse stuck his arm out between the bars to shake Garfield's hand. "I'm not in any mood for bullshit. Get me out of here."

"Can you make bail?"

"What's that mean?"

"Pay. Can you pay?"

"I'll have to call my uncle. He's loaded."

Garfield nodded. "Your bond hearing is at 10 a.m., they all are, so we might have to wait 'til your name is called."

"How much will it cost to get me out of here?"

"That's up to the judge. Assaulting a police officer is no laughing matter."

"Who's laughing?"

Garfield turned to Keith. "Can we have a minute? I don't want to make my client look stupid in front of his friend."

Jesse took offense. "Hey, I'm right here."

Keith grinned. "Sure." He left.

"Mr. Curley."

"Call me Jesse."

"Okay, Jesse." Garfield scratched his head. "The charges against you are serious."

"They're phony. I never touched him. Not a hair."

"It's his word against yours, and the DA's office always takes the cop's side. We might get lucky, knock it down to a misdemeanor. Do you have any priors?"

"No, sir. I'm in uncharted territory here."

"Yeah. First time's always the toughest. However, before we can claim police brutality or false imprisonment, we've got to get through this bond hearing. Then I'll review the evidence, it's called discovery. From there, we can plot a defense."

Jesse grabbed the bars. He was getting good at it. "I'll tell you this much, there's something wrong with Kellerman. He's unprofessional and goes off half-cocked like he's bipolar or something. You need to check him out."

"All that can come later."

"He was in the NYPD."

"Okay. Chin up." He checked his watch like he had to catch a bus. "See you at 10 a.m."

***

They came for Jesse at 9:30, two deputy sheriffs in tan uniforms and armed with Billy Clubs and mace. Handcuffed and shackled, he was escorted to an elevator and taken down to the city courthouse. The small room had five rows of seats, like church pews, two long tables for the litigants, and a table up front, on a raised platform, for the judge, currently absent. Upright flags, the Stars and Stripes on the right, and the dark blue New York state flag on the left, stood against a paneled wall behind the platform. A woman in a business suit sat at a desk off to the side marked CLERK, and twelve chairs in the jury box stood empty. Officer Keith Clarkson sat in the front row of pews. His mom and Uncle Francis sat behind him. The asshole Kellerman, his accuser, was nowhere in sight.

Jesse's shackles clinked and clanked as the deputies led him to the table on the left and sat him in a hard wooden chair. He glanced back at his mom. She looked terrified.

Paul Garfield arrived, sat in a cushy chair beside him, opened his briefcase on the table and removed a bunch of legal papers. "Charging documents," he whispered.

All lies. "What are my chances of getting out of this?"

"Keep your voice down."

A man in a blue suit, his hair slicked back mobster style, strode in, his patent-leather shoes clicking on the hardwood floor all the way to the opposing table where he sat and smirked at Garfield and Jesse.

"Who's that?"

"Assistant DA Matt Johnson," Paul whispered. "A real prick. Don't say anything to piss him off."

A deputy stepped up beside the judge's table. "All rise for the Honorable Judge Delaney."

Everyone stood as the judge, wearing a clichéd black robe, entered from a rear door and sat in a plush high-backed chair behind his table. "Mornin' all." He adjusted his glasses. "I see everyone is present for this bond hearing."

Jesse rubbed his clammy hands on his pants. His mouth felt so dry he could spit sand.

The bailiff approached the judge and handed him a file folder. "Docket number 4223. People versus Jesse Curley. The charge is an assault against a police officer."

The judge opened the folder and gave the

contents a quick read through then looked up. "Counselor," he addressed Garfield. "Is your client aware of the severity of this charge?"

Garfield stood. "Yes, your honor."

"I'm not guilty," Jesse put in.

The judge banged his gavel. "I'll have no more outbursts from you, sir. This is not the time or place to make a plea. We're here to determine whether or not you'll be released on bond. Mr. Garfield, what do you propose?"

"We request Mr. Curley be released on his own recognizance, your Honor."

"Mr. Johnson..." He addressed the ADA. "Does the state concur?"

Johnson stood. "No, your Honor. Considering the heinous attack on a Peekskill police officer by the defendant, the state requests a fifty thousand cash security bond and ankle bracelet monitoring."

Yup. He's a prick, alright. Jesse seethed.

Garfield countered. "Come off it, Matt.." He raised a sheet of paper from the briefcase. "I've got Mr. Curley's financial statement right here. He doesn't have two nickels to rub together. He has no priors, and his sister is in the ICU at Hudson Valley. He's not a flight risk."

Keith stood. "If it pleases the court. I can vouch

for him."

The judge nodded. "Thank you, Officer Clarkson." He set his gaze on the prosecutor. "Seems the defense counsel has a valid point."

"The state stands firm, your Honor."

"Why are you being so hardnosed about this?"

"We believe he's a threat to the community, and as we speak, he's under investigation for attempted bank robbery, as well."

"Objection," Garfield shouted. "Irrelevant. The court should know that if my client can't make bail, he'll not be able to see his sister, who's near death from a knife attack behind the Bliss Nightclub."

"Objection," Johnson yelled. "Irrelevant."

At that, the judge addressed Jesse directly. "That was your sister?"

"Yes, sir...ah...your Honor. I have to get out of here."

"Your, Honor..." Johnson interjected. "Don't fall for his sad-sack pleadings. The state prefers to keep him confined until trial. Our police force deserves to be protected."

The judge banged his gavel. "That's an overreach, Johnson. Miss Billings," he addressed the clerk, "set this matter for arraignment at the earliest convenience. Mr. Curley, you're free to go on your word you'll be present for all proceedings in this case. Don't make me regret my decision."

Garfield nodded. "Thank you, your Honor." He glanced at Johnson and smirked.

Johnson scowled. "This ain't over, Paul. In the end, your boy is going to prison."

"Good luck with that." Garfield closed his briefcase. "We'll be ready."

The deputies got Jesse to his feet, unlocked the handcuffs and shackles. He looked back to see the smiling faces of his mom and uncle. Kellerman was still MIA.

I'm going to get that son of a bitch if it's the last thing I do.

***

Jesse couldn't get to the hospital fast enough, but considering all the trouble he was in, he didn't chance a speeding ticket. He could finally breathe again, free of the jail cell, the handcuffs, and a system of justice that was more bent on 'winning' than the truth. Garfield had done a great job at the bond hearing; he deserved every tax-payer dollar he earned. Still, a bigger battle loomed, the arraignment and trial.

He arrived at Hudson Valley ICU. His mom and uncle had gotten there first, probably broke the speed limit to do it. She jumped up from a waiting room chair to hug him. "Oh, Jesse..." she hesitated to inspect the lump on the side of his head, barely visible under his hair, but a mother never misses her child's injury. "What happened to you?" She had to go and touch it.

"Ouch." He recoiled. "It's nothing, Mom."

"I don't believe that, not for a second. You're in some kind of trouble... Have you been gambling again?"

"It's nothing I can't handle."

"That's what you always say."

"Mom, drop it."

"Ever since you lost your job at Vericom, bad things started happening to you. How would your father react if he could see you in all this trouble?"

"He wouldn't be happy, I'm sure. What's your point?"

She shuddered. "Seems like our family is cursed. First your dad gets murdered, now your sister..." she sobbed, "near death. Dear God, how much more can we take?"

Jesse hugged her tightly. "We're going to be alright. I have to believe that or go completely insane."

"I just want my baby back."

"Let's go in and see her." He nodded to the duty

nurse.

She pushed the button to open the doors to ICU.

Jesse followed his mother and uncle to curtain number two. Nothing had changed, the same mummy wrappings, the same machines, the same rhythmic pulse of the rasping ventilator. A nurse was with her, looking glum.

"Is she any better? Something we can't see, like in her brain, her internal injuries healing? Anything to hang our hopes on?"

"Her kidneys are working." She indicated the urine drainage bag hanging from a lower bed rail. "She's getting another MRI this afternoon to get a look at her brain swell. After that, the doctor may be able to tell you more."

"Oh my God, it's horrible." Mom's cheeks flushed. "I hope they catch the animal who did this." She held her daughter's hand. "We're here for you, baby. We all love you. Come back to us."

Jesse couldn't bear to watch all this sorrow any longer. He couldn't just stand by and do nothing. "I gotta go, Mom."

She gasped. "Where?"

"Clarissa's would-be killer is still out there, and I aim to find him before anything else goes wrong."

"Be careful."

He bent over his sister. "Hang in there, okay? There's nobody tougher than you. I love you, sis."

He turned and walked out. Family curse or no curse, he had to start somewhere, and that would be the Bliss.

***

Nick Fortune's day started much the same as usual, opening the club at 9 a.m. and counting receipts from the night before. His staff arrived on time, two barmaids who went about the tables, setting the chairs on the floor, and the bartender, slicing oranges and limes, and spooning maraschino cherries from a jar.

Ceiling lights lit the barroom, the dance floor, and the empty DJ booth, giving the place a totally different ambiance than the nighttime crowd enjoyed. No flashing strobes, no brilliant neon, no loud music...and patrons from a different class of folks wandered in, the early morning drinkers yearning to numb their senses and, by noon, sleep the bender off under a bridge somewhere.

Fortune also had the unenviable job of barback. He toted buckets of ice from the downstairs ice machine, checked beer kegs in the cooler that fed the taps along the back bar, and hauled cases of bottled beer to the refrigerators under the bar-top. The inventory of all the liquor and wine wasn't backbreaking work, but tedious just the same.

However, this morning was different in one compelling way. Detective Kellerman's visit last night and the video of the assault on that poor young woman, wore on his mind. Over the years, since he'd purchased the Bliss, he'd had many interactions with people: patrons, liquor reps, beer delivery drivers, but very little involvement with the police. A handshake often determined his first impression of someone. Kellerman's hand had a slimy feel to it, sweaty, *and I couldn't wipe my palm on my pants fast enough.* And his resemblance in body size and stature to the attacker was uncanny, not just an off-the-cuff observation. He decided, as soon as he could, to watch the video again.

Maybe I missed something.

Until then, there were cases of beer to lug, ice to haul, and floors to mop.

***

Jesse drove toward the Bliss, always on the lookout for Conrad, as he wouldn't be put off much longer. Next time a confrontation with him wouldn't end with a lump on the head but a cracking of leg bones. He shuddered.

What he needed was a job and information from

the Bliss, a look at their security video, most importantly, and the opportunity to talk to witnesses. Problem was, posing questions like a reporter might alienate people who just want to mind their own business. He couldn't rely on the police or Kellerman to come forward with any clues, especially after his arrest for assault. He was on his own.

Arriving at the club, he parked out front, next to a black Mercedes E350 sedan, ran his fingers through his hair, and used the cracked vanity mirror to check for any wild hairs in his nose. He could only hope his clothes didn't look too much slept in, and that the owner or manager wouldn't conduct a background check and discover his recent arrest.

Not a good look.

He strode into the club, head high and chest out.

Stay confident. Be yourself.

Inside a few steps, he stopped and looked around for anyone who appeared important. It was a little before noon. Several men were seated at the bar, and a janitor, mopping the floor, eyed him. "You lost, boy?"

"Do you know where I can find the owner?"

"You're looking at him. What do you want?"

"You're Nick Fortune?"

"The one and the only. Who are you?"

"Jesse. Jesse Curley."

Shock etched deep lines in Fortune's brow. "You any relation to the girl—"

"My sister."

"Are you looking for trouble?"

"No, sir. A job." He indicated the mop. "I'm sure you have better things to do than mop the floor."

He leaned on the mop handle and tweaked his eyebrows as if contemplating that possibility.

"I can swing a mop, take out the trash, stack beer cases, you name it."

"Is that right? Ever been a barback?"

"No, but I'm a quick learner."

"It's an ass-busting job to back the bartender, lugging cases of beer, buckets of ice, doing all the grunt work while he gets to chat it up with the ladies."

"I'm not interested in my social life. Give me a shot at being a barback."

Fortune stuffed the mop into the bucket. "Come to think of it, I've got some video footage to look at..." he glanced at his watch. "You see that door behind the bar?"

On a wall of shelved liquor bottles, the door wasn't hard to spot. He nodded. "What about it?"

"Go through that door and run down the stairs

to the basement. Grab a case of beer, any beer, and carry it up to the bar."

He shrugged. "Can't be all that hard."

"You have one minute."

"One minute?"

Fortune viewed his watch. "Yes. You ready?"

I'm not, but I need this job.

"Yes, sir."

"Go," Fortune shouted.

Jesse booked past Fortune, skidded around the bar, and flew through the door to thunder down the steps. In the brightly lit basement, he stopped short to inspect a row of dark monitors, possibly connected to a surveillance computer... But for now, *where's the beer?*

"Thirty seconds," Fortune shouted from the door above.

He spotted cases of liquor and wine stacked along the near wall. Hay bales along the far wall seemed out of place. He rushed to a lighted cooler, threw open a door, and snatched up the nearest case of beer.

"Ten seconds."

Bottles clinking, he juggled it up the stairs and set it on the bar, heart pounding. "How did...I do?" He was gasping for breath.

Fortune, standing on the other side of the bar, frowned as he checked his watch then regarded Jesse with that same scowl of disapproval. "You're five seconds late and just cost me money."

"Five seconds?"

He glanced at the mop bucket and the wet floor, then shrugged. "Well...it's good enough, but remember, every second is important. Slow-flowing liquor and beer means unhappy drinkers in a crowded bar. They'll take their business elsewhere."

There is hope after all. "Great, how much?"

"What do you mean, how much?"

"Pay, wages, hourly, you know?"

"Are you for real? Consider yourself lucky to have a job."

"Okay." He placed a finger on his chin. "I've considered it. Thank you. Now, how much?"

"Smartass, huh?"

"My good looks never got me anywhere."

"How about fifty bucks a week?"

Jesse glanced at the bartender who was shaking his head no.

"Make it one fifty and my share of the tips."

"One fifty? That's larceny."

Jesse tipped his head to the mop bucket and shrugged. "Your choice."

From the tilt of his brows, it was clear that Fortune had gotten the message. "Alright, but you start right now." He retrieved the mop and shoved it in Jesse's hand.

He grinned.

Now to break into that security computer.

Chapter Thirteen

Meanwhile, back in the ICU, Clarissa lay in her vegetative state. Jude and Francis continued their bedside vigil, taking turns holding her bandaged hand from which only three fingers protruded. It seemed this heartbreak would never end...until the nurse came in to check on her.

On a cursory glance at the machines surrounding the bed, she gasped.

"What is it?" Jude asked in alarm.

"The EEG...my God. Look at the EEG."

Jude examined the screen, had no idea what she was looking at, just some squiggly lines.

"There's accelerated brain activity." Karen's heart raced. "I'm getting the doctor." She rushed out to the hallway.

"Paging Doctor Anderson, bed two. Stat."

A doctor hurried in, looked over the machines, checked data print-outs, and nodded. "This is encouraging. Let's get her to imaging. An MRI should confirm reduced swelling in her brain."

"What does that mean," she asked, hopeful but

guarded.

"I think it's time to bring her out of the coma."

"She's going to be okay. My God, it's a miracle."

"Not so fast. We have no idea what damage her brain has sustained. For all we know, she could remain in a comatose state for months, maybe years. If she regains consciousness, we'll need to run some cognitive and motor skill tests. She's by no means out of the woods."

Jude fell into her brother's arms. "I have to believe she's going to pull through."

He patted her back. "She's gotten this far. Keep the faith, girl."

The nurse pulled the curtains full-open, and an orderly wheeled Clarissa out of the ICU toward an uncertain prognosis.

***

During the afternoon lull at the Bliss, Nick Fortune summoned Jesse to the bar where he was taking a break, nursing a Gin and Tonic. His hand trembled every time he lifted the tumbler to his lips.

"Are you okay?" Jesse asked.

Fortune pointed to the vacant stool beside him. "Sit."

"You're not going to fire me already, are you?"

"You say you're an IT guy laid off from

Vericom."

"Yeah. Jobs like that are hard to come by."

He slammed the dregs of his drink and sucked on an ice cube, thinking. Jesse saw dread in his boss's eyes. "What's going on?"

"I fought in Iraq and Afghanistan, but I never knew fear like this." He slid the glass to the bartender. "Top it off."

As the bartender refreshed the drink, Fortune turned to Jesse. "I made a big mistake...totally misjudged Detective Kellerman when I told him he looked a lot like your sister's attacker."

Jesse raised his eyebrows. "You saw the video?"

"Watched it over and over. It's maddening."

"Actually, I was hoping to get a look at it."

The bartender delivered the new drink then returned to his bar-keeping duties, washing glasses.

Fortune glanced at the tumbler but left it on the bar. "I want you to see it, so you know what I know...what Kellerman knows I know."

"Why me?"

"You're her brother. You have a vested interest." He pulled a gun from his waistband and raised the barrel to the ceiling. "I carry this with me every day. Now I've got to sleep with it every night."

Jesse eyed the gun, wondered if he should have

one of his own. "You think Kellerman's out to kill you?"

"Come on." He stood and parked the gun behind his belt. "I'll show you why." He downed the drink then led the way around the bar to the door and down the stairs.

The lined up monitors were all in sleep mode, but oddly, against the far wall, in front of the hay bales, three mannequins were also lined up. One male dressed in business attire, a bald guy in a polo and slacks, and the third, a Yankee fan, ball cap and all.

Jesse wondered what they were doing down there, but before he could ask, Fortune drew his gun and popped all three of them dead center mass. Jesse's ears rang, and the stink of cordite floated in the smoky air. "Jesus, man. What the fuck?"

"Since I left the army, I've kept my skills sharp, and target shooting is a bore."

"Looks like you're a pretty good shot."

He tucked the gun away. "I rarely miss."

"I'll keep that in mind."

Fortune laughed and clapped his hands three times. The monitors flashed to a white background with black numbers in the center, counting down from 30...29...28...

"Activate."

The desktop icons appeared, and the peripheral monitors showed camera views from around the bar, inside and out, six to a screen.

"Wow. I'm impressed."

"Spared no expense." He offered Jesse a chair and they sat together while Fortune clicked here and there until a video came up. "I've condensed hours worth into a couple clips." He clicked the triangular PLAY icon. There was Clarissa, alright, dancing with some Saturday-Night-Fever looking guy. She appeared to like him a lot, by the way the were going at it. The clip ended. "Did you see it?"

"I saw her dancing...so?"

"Me too, a hundred times, and the back alley video, as well. I kept asking myself, where did he come from? How did he know your sister had gone out back? Was he just some lone wolf out for a random victim, or did he target her?"

"Clarissa? She didn't have an enemy in the world."

He reversed the video. "Look at it again, but don't watch her, watch the crowd." PLAY.

There was no sound but lots of motion, too much to keep track of, faces turning, bodies jumping in unison.

"There." He hit PAUSE. "Do you see it?"

Jesse studied the frozen image, somewhat blurred, scanned the crowd, though his gaze kept going back to Clarissa, her hair stopped in mid-flight, the smile on her face frozen, and the sparkle in her eye still evident. "What am I supposed to...?

And then he saw it, back in the shadows, at a table behind other tables...in the background between two patrons, the unmistakable mug of Harry Kellerman. "Son of a bitch. He was there the whole time."

"Yeah. I thought that was strange, can't really tell what he's wearing, scanned every video, but he didn't show up again, so I started doubting my own eyes."

"Let's see the video of the assault."

"No way. You don't want to see that, but I assure you, the masked assailant looks like Kellerman in size and by the way he walks."

"Then that's it? Not very compelling."

"Ah-hah, that's where you're mistaken, and what I'm going to show you next is something I'm sure Kellerman would kill to keep out of the investigation."

PLAY.

"Here's where he arrives at the crime scene, twenty minutes later. As you watch, you'll see it's positively him."

The video was grainy from the low light, but flashing police car lights gave the scene a strobing effect. Grainy. Sharp. Grainy. Sharp. Jesse watched Kellerman walk about, squat down, stand up, walk around until he moved out of sight down the passageway between the buildings. "I see a detective scoping out the scene."

PAUSE. REWIND. PLAY.

"Watch when he stoops...right here...his right hand clearly visible, but when he stands...look at his right hand now."

PAUSE.

"It's in his pocket." Jesse gasped. "What the hell? He picked up something."

"He compromised the crime scene, removed evidence. And I think I know what he took."

REWIND. PLAY.

"Watch the ground at his feet. Every time a police light flashes, see...the glint...there it is again...glint...but when he stands...no glint. Nothing."

Jesse's throat tightened. "A piece of glass?"

"Close. During the video of the assault, it's clear that your sister put up a fight, and at one point, she picked up a broken bottle neck. She was down, but she swiped it at her attacker, and damned if she didn't slice his leg...that's what it looked like. He backed up a step, so I'm sure she got him a good one."

Now Jesse saw the full picture. "It had his blood on it."

"That's what I think, and if he sees this, he'll know I've seen it, and that's why he'll kill me...to keep me from talking." He shut down the security system. "Jesse, if anything happens to me, you'll know who's responsible and why."

"Son of a bitch. What are you going to do?"

"Go to the station, talk to his boss, his higher-up, his captain, whomever, and show him this." He held up a flash drive. "I'm not going down without a fight." He set it on the table, stood, drew the gun, and blasted another bullet hole in each of the dummies along the far wall.

Jesse cupped his hands over his ears. If he was a gambling man, which he was, odds of Fortune nailing Kellerman would definitely interest Conrad. All hell was going to break loose.

***

That afternoon, as Kellerman did three times a week, he made the heartbreaking drive to the Hudson Valley Children's Sanctum. The tree-lined entrance road, dappled with sunlight, was the last bit of peace he'd have before he, again, faced the horrible reality that his life, and Deirdre's, had become.

At the front door he hesitated, as he did every time he stood there, fearing to go inside. His hands trembled and his heart thumped with despair, but the anger he had to keep to himself. He took five deliberate breaths and opened the door. The first step, and again, with each step inside, he questioned why God had chosen all these children to suffer when they should be out playing with their friends. Where was God when He mattered most to those who needed him most?

He checked in at the front desk, and as always, he received a PARENT'S PASS, and he knew where to go without instruction, down the hall, to the left, third room on the right. The brightly painted walls that resembled sunshine felt more like cold gray brick. When he arrived at her room, decorated in flowers and stuffed animals with perpetual smiles, his daughter wasn't there, which gave him a start.

Nurse Sarah Franklin, a black-haired woman, a saint in her own right, with readers hanging on a cord from her neck, paced toward him, her tennis shoes squeaking on the tile floor. "Good afternoon, Harold." Again came the cheeriest smile she could muster. Around here they called him Harold Dodson, though he preferred Harry, as in Dirty Harry, as in justice at any cost. "Where is she?"

She stopped in front of him, a little closer than he felt comfortable with, but friendly enough. "Outside, playing with her friends."

"Playing?"

"You know playing here is not like playing everywhere, but it's still playing to these children."

He rubbed his temple. "How do you do it? Day in and day out, 24/7, dealing with the heartbreak here, knowing these kids will never get better in this mausoleum of a hospital. It takes a special person not to despair when there's no progress, no hope."

"I see progress. Little things, like a twitch of a finger or the wiggle of a toe. A little smile could make my day, gives me hope to see one some day. I'm surprised you don't see that, Harold."

"My job is to ruin people's lives. Lock them up. Destroy their hopes and dreams. But even then, some criminals can be rehabilitated. For these kids...never..." He felt the sting of a fresh tear. "There's no reprieve."

"I understand. This job isn't for everyone. Nor is yours."

"There's no comparison."

"I don't quit. I don't lose hope. I strive for progress. Go see your daughter and remember what I just said."

Kellerman, feeling whipped with a morality stick, plodded, head down, to the hospital's backyard. There, a multi-colored playground basked in the sunshine, such a sad sight with no children on the swings or sliding down the slide. The merry-go-round stood in deathly silence, as did the childish laughter that no one ever heard around here.

To his right, under a shade tree, a group of children in wheelchairs formed a circle. In the center, a nurse, overly joyous amid all the gloom, clapped her hands. "Okay, kids. Let's sing Old Macdonald," and began: "Old Macdonald had a farm..." Her voice was the only voice to rise from the circle. "E-i-e-i-o."

A dark shadow enveloped the play area, a cloud floating by, maybe even death itself, looming over many of these kids who were immune to the treatments and rehabilitation efforts of the staff. Like Deirdre.

"And on this farm he had a cow..."

Standing there, he spotted her in the wheelchair, strapped in straight and tight, but her head lolled over and her eyes were a blank stare. Nothing would get through to her, not *Old MacDonald* nor the joyous *e-i-e-i-o*. He wished he could help her, escape with her to Disneyland or Magic Mountain, someplace with ice cream, cake, and candy...progress, hope, and happiness every little girl deserved. Not this hell on earth delivered at the supersonic speed of flying lead.

For Christ's sake, this is my child. Why her, God, why?

Fighting a total meltdown, he waited for the nurse to end the song before approaching closer. She spotted him right away, brightened and knelt to his daughter's wheelchair. "Your dad's here, Deirdre. Isn't that good news?"

No response, not a twitch of a finger or the wiggle of a toe. The nurse wheeled her to a nearby bench under a gazebo and he joined them there. His heart pumped hopelessness, as he was now close enough to hear the pop and wheeze of the portable ventilator, strapped to the chair back, that kept her alive, and the beeping of monitors that proved she wasn't dead, the physical incarnation of his nightmares.

"She's having a good day, Mr. Dodson." The nurse set the brake on the wheelchair. "The fresh air is good for her."

"She looks the same every day."

"I'll leave you two alone to have a nice chat."

He sank to the bench and looked at her face, gaunt now, her blank staring eyes greasy with protective ointment. Her head was tilted almost to her shoulder, and the corrugated tube in her throat was taped to her neck for fear it might come loose. Mouth agape, drool escaped her limp lips and leaked down onto the bib she wore. Her wrists were bent and her hands were curled, her arms adducted and flexed against her chest, her feet turned inward and her toes pointed down, all indicative of sever brain injury posturing.

Could she hear? Did she see? Nobody knew.

He leaned forward. "Hey, pumpkin, how are you doing today?"

"*I missed you, Daddy.*" Her voice was soft as cotton candy, angelic in his mind, but her frozen, dull expression never faltered.

Tears burned his eyes. "I missed you, too, sweetheart." He clutched her cold, clawed hand. "I hope you can hear me. Can you hear me? If you can, squeeze my finger."

Nothing.

"Can you blink?"

Nothing but drool and the incessant *pop and wheeze*.

"Remember how you knocked down three-pointers on the *basketball* court, how you dreamed of being a high school *basketball* star, how you hoped the scouts would recruit you for a *basketball* scholarship to college? *Basketball.* Do you remember your love for *basketball*?"

He'd hoped, as he'd hoped every time, the word basketball would get a reaction, any reaction from her, a smile, a twitch, but like every time before, he got no response. The same wooden look, the same cold stare.

"Mom and I love you."

"My mom is dead!"

The anger in her voice unnerved him, but in a way, Kathleen was murdered by that same bullet that crippled their child, only it killed her a lot quicker...by her own hand...with his service weapon, left on the kitchen table, unknowing, unfeeling, uncaring about what she would use it for. As much as he wanted to blame that gun, he knew it was her fault for checking out the way she did.

His blood heated with a spike of adrenaline, to a boil, it seemed. "They're all going to pay for ruining our family, honey."

"Like Seamus Curley paid?"

"I made him pay first, gunned him down like a mad dog while he sat in his patrol car. He got what he had coming. And now his daughter is on life support, not long for this world."

"When is it going to be enough, Daddy?"

He didn't like her accusatory tone. "Enough?" Anger flared deep in his chest, like an iron fist clutching his heart. "How many times do I have to tell you? The Curleys did this to us. There's one more left, and his death will be the most gruesome of all."

"Not so loud, Daddy. They will hear you."

He clamped his mouth shut, looked around, saw only zombie kids who might have heard his outburst. Two nurses stood by the door, ever vigilant but out of earshot, for sure.

Veins throbbed in his neck. A month after the shooting, he and Kathleen...their marriage began to implode. The arguments never ceased, and divorce became inevitable.

"That's not our daughter anymore," she had said, bashing his chest with the blunt of her fist. "It's some imposter."

"She's still our daughter. She deserves our love, our care. It's not her fault."

Kathleen dug her fingers into her temples, her anguish palpable. "She can't speak. She doesn't know me."

"You can't give up on her."

"There's nothing inside her. A shell. A vegetable. Can't you see that? Her heart beats, but that infernal thumping machine keeps her alive."

"She might come out of it someday."

Her face flushed. "What about the cop who shot her? Accidental? What a joke. Make him pay, honey." She dropped to her knees, bawling. "I can't live like this anymore."

"Don't say that."

"It's too much."

The sudden recall of an echoing gunshot brought him back to his seat on the bench and the *pop* and *wheeze* from Deirdre's chair. He gripped her hand. Drool trickled out of her mouth, an endless seep of misery that fed his psychosis.

"I love you, Daddy."

What cruel tricks a battered mind does play.

He leaned in and kissed her on the forehead. "I'll be back soon, baby. Hang in there."

He had to finish this, once and for all.

Chapter Fourteen

Clarissa opened her eyes to a bleary scene, haloed lights, and strange noises that echoed from a long tunnel. She blinked. *Am I dead?*

Glimpses of loved ones lingered in her brain like remnants of a dream. Then came a nightmare, the fight for her life in the alley, the masked man...the knife. She gasped. Her throat felt raw and bruised...

"There you are," a man's voice said, hollow and far away. "Welcome back to the world."

Huh?

"Clarissa, honey. It's a miracle."

Mom?

"I told you she'd be alright."

Uncle Francis?

"How do you feel?" the man's voice again, his ghostly form above her, a light flashing in her left eye...then her right. A flashlight? A doctor?

"Where am I?" Something wasn't right. She didn't hear her voice ask the question. There was something wrong with her throat. *"What's wrong with me?"* Nothing came out. *"Help."*

She trashed and kicked at bed sheets.

"Now, now" a woman's voice said, a nurse, Clarissa realized, standing over her. "Take it easy. You've been through a lot."

Clarissa coughed, her throat was so dry. *"Water."* Still nothing. She hacked.

"Here, sip this water." The nurse poked a straw at Clarissa's lips.

She sipped and choked.

"Not so fast."

"God. I'm so thirsty."

"A little. Go slow. Your throat and trachea are bound to be sore from the ventilator tube. Swallowing will be difficult."

I was on a ventilator? "How long have I been out?" Her mouth moved, but no sound came out.

The doctor's form returned, a little clearer this time, enough that she could make out his white hair and glasses... "Miss Curley, this may be difficult, but I want to test your responses to establish a baseline on which to gage your recovery progress. Is that okay?"

She nodded, painful as it was to move her head, and patted her throat.

"I know you can't speak, perfectly normal, just bear with me. Can you follow my finger with your eyes?"

She forced her eyes to focus. They felt lazy and disobedient, but she managed to see his finger moving back and forth.

Then he tapped her nose.

She blinked.

He pulled up the sheet and flicked a finger at her toe. "Did you feel that?'

She nodded.

He gripped her hand. "Squeeze my hand as hard as you can."

She felt his hand, its warmth and its strength, and she thought she squeezed it pretty hard.

"Good." He stepped back. "That's all for now. You need to build up your strength." He turned to the nurse. "Get her some Jell-O. Maybe by dinnertime, she can eat something soft, mashed potatoes and meatloaf."

"I'll help her try to get it down."

"Wait. How long has it been since I've eaten?"

She didn't feel hungry, mostly just woozy, took the opportunity to close her eyes.

***

Kellerman's phone rang while he drove on Route 9 toward the station. *Peekskill Police* showed on the display. "Kellerman."

"Detective. The hospital called. Clarissa Curley

has come out of the coma."

His pulse shot up. "Did she say anything?"

"She's awake is all I know."

"I'm on my way there."

"10-4."

He turned on the misery lights, gunned the gas, and sped up Route 9, curious about her reaction when she saw him. Would she recognize him before he pressed a pillow to her face? He could only hope she wouldn't scream. Blasting through red lights on Crompond, he reached the hospital entrance in short order.

He parked and hustled to the lobby elevator. On the ride up to the ICU, he wondered how much she could tell him about the attack.

At the ICU nurses' station, he flashed his badge. "Let me in to see Clarissa Curley."

The duty nurse frowned. "She's not able to speak yet."

"That's alright. I'll get what I need."

"Suit yourself." She tapped the button, and the doors levered open.

He marched in and stopped at the gap in the curtain around bed number two where he lingered to observe the goings-on within. Most of the machines had been removed from around the bed, leaving more room for relatives to be near. The mother was holding the girl's hand. He stepped in behind them and cleared his throat.

They turned in surprise. "Oh, detective," Jude said.

"I hate to intrude, but I heard the good news."

"Isn't it amazing?"

"I must talk to her."

"Tomorrow," Uncle Francis said. "She's resting."

"I don't have that luxury. You want me to solve this case, or not?"

"Of course we do," Jude put in.

"Then step aside. I won't be long."

The nurse walked in. "Jude, Francis, let's go down the hall, find some coffee. We'll let the detective do his job."

"She can't tell you anything," Jude said.

"We'll see." He pulled a notepad from his jacket.

The nurse nudged Clarissa. "Wake up, honey. You have a visitor."

Her eyes opened and locked on him.

He smiled at her. *No sign of recognition.*

"We'll be back in a couple minutes." The nurse herded them out, leaving Kellerman alone. He loomed over her, his fingers curling, his eyes assessing the pillow against the headboard, the position of her face. Easy peasy.

#

Clarissa stared up at the looming hulk of a man. Her parched tongue glided over her lips. *"Who are you?"* Talking was useless.

The big man held a notepad. "Miss Curley, I'm Detective Kellerman with the Peekskill Police. I'd like to ask you a few questions."

She put a finger on her throat and coughed.

"I've been told you can't speak, so to start, I'll ask questions that require a yes or no answer. Nod for yes, shake your head for no."

She stared at his eyes, chilled, but she didn't know why.

"About your attacker, was he tall?"

Still staring, she nodded and pointed at him.

"My height?"

She nodded.

"How about his build, lanky?"

"Big." Only able to rasp, she pointed to him.

"Big, like me?"

She reached for her water bottle on the bedside table.

He handed it to her.

Holding it between her wrists, she sipped from the straw and fought an eerie feeling that didn't make

---

sense.

It can't be him. He's a cop.

He took the water bottle, set it aside, and offered her his notepad. "Perhaps you could write something down that might be helpful."

As she struggled to hold the pad with the free fingers of her bandaged left hand, he set a pen between two fingers of her right hand. While juggling this impossible task, she saw him grab the pillow, hold it with both hands, and move closer. Terror lit fires in her bloodstream. *What's he doing? Is he going to smother me? Kill me?* "Nurse." It came out as a grunt. The pillow came closer, now casting a shadow on her face.

The heart monitor beeped frantically.

A nurse rushed in. "You're upsetting her, detective."

He turned around, brows furrowed, still holding the pillow in both hands.

"*Help. He's gonna kill me.*" Grunt, groan, grunt.

The nurse gasped. "What are you doing with that pillow?"

"Fluffing it up." He demonstrated by squeezing it. "I was going to put it under her head, prop her up a bit so she can write in my notepad."

"*He's lying. He's lying.*" Unintelligible rasping

came out.

The nurse snatched the notebook and pen from her, then slapped them into Kellerman's hand. "Does she really look like she can write anything?"

"She needs to try—"

"She needs her rest. Time for you to leave, detective."

He turned to Clarissa. "See you real soon."

She shook her head no.

The nurse escorted him away, and her mom and uncle strode in like all was now right with the world.

"Get me out of here. He's coming back to kill me."

Chapter Fifteen

Nick Fortune was on a mission to take down the new homicide detective, Kellerman. Armed with the flash drive loaded with his security video, he drove to police headquarters on Nelson, and parked in the public garage across the street. He hoped the precinct captain would hear his case and watch the department's new cop in action.

He descended the precinct steps, scanning for Kellerman. He hadn't taken kindly to being told he looked like the guy in the alley. Fortune was sure the clip of him in the bar and when he picked up the bottleneck from the crime scene, would put a nail in his coffin. Until then, Fortune knew his life was in danger.

Inside, at the duty desk, the sergeant glanced up from his paperwork. "What can I do for you?"

"I'd like to see the captain."

"Come on, buddy. There's more than one captain here. What department?"

"Homicide or Major Crimes, whichever you call it."

"What did you do, kill somebody?"

"I have information about a case, the Clarissa Curley assault." He held up the flash drive.

"I'll call Detective Kellerman down. It's his case."

"No. No. No. The captain. Only he can see the video I have here."

"He's the only one available." The sergeant leaned forward. "If you got something important, he'll want to see it."

Before Fortune could plead his case further, Kellerman pushed through the door behind the sergeant. "What's going on here?"

Shit.

"On second thought, it's not that important." Fortune turned and sprinted for the door.

"Wait," the sergeant shouted.

Outside, Fortune bounded up the steps to the sidewalk and darted across the street to the parking garage. There, he looked back to see if anyone was chasing him. He'd made Kellerman suspicious, and the dogged cop would certainly not let it slide.

He's coming for me now, for sure.

Fortune jumped in his car and headed back to the Bliss at breakneck speed.

***

Kellerman stood beside the Duty Sergeant.

"What did he want?"

"He had a flash drive with video about the Clarissa Curley case, but he didn't want you to see it. Asked for the captain. Why would he say that?"

Because he suspects me.

"Because he knows I'm on to him. I plan to make an arrest pretty soon."

***

Nick Fortune slammed the butt of his fist on the steering wheel as he sped from the police station. That was a stupid thing to do, go to the cops with evidence of a maniac in their midst. *I've raised his suspicions, big time. Nice going, Nick.* His stomach rolled with dread.

His cell phone rang, and he glanced down. *Peekskill Police.* Kellerman? *I'll bet he's eager to find out what I know.* "I know everything," he muttered but dared not answer. The call went to voicemail. Distracted from his driving for only a second, the blare of a tractor-trailer made him look up. *Shit.* He'd veered over the center line and about got creamed. What he wouldn't give to be back in Fallujah, right now, where he was safer.

After a four-mile drive to the outskirts of town, he screeched into the Bliss parking lot, claimed his reserved spot, and bailed out of the Mercedes. His phone chirped a new voicemail. He pushed PLAY and listened.

"Mr. Fortune, it's Detective Kellerman. I understand you have that flash drive containing the Clarissa Curley videos. Return to the station with it as soon as possible. I'll also need a formal statement from you about the origin of the video to authenticate it. Thank you for your cooperation."

"You lying son of a bitch." He saved the message and rushed inside. The bartender was preparing for a busy night.

"Where's your new barback?"

"He's at the hospital. His sister woke up."

"Peachy." Fortune sent him a text. *"Something's come up. I need you to come in early, cover for me. Busy night. Half-price drinks for the ladies. The bartender is slammed. Oh, and good news about your sister."*

A text chimed in. *Kellerman.*

"Get your ass in here or I'll send a posse to drag you in."

Nick was never hard to find, spent most of his time at the Bliss... He made note of the afternoon patrons: Billy from the garage on his usual barstool, Carrie the Molly Maid, a gaggle of secretaries, Ginger and Sylvia the barmaids...this was no place to make a stand against Kellerman. Someone could get hurt.

He'd be better off hold up in his apartment, top floor, one way in, one way out. *I don't dare hang around here another minute.*

He rushed downstairs and unlocked his security computer. In case anything happened to him, Jesse would have access to all the footage. The IT guy would know what to do with it.

In the corner, an old ARMY trunk held his keepsakes from Iraq: four boxes of 9mm ammo, two 15-round clips, his M9 service pistol, a beret, desert fatigues, and rummaging through it, he came up with an M67 fragmentation grenade he'd secreted to the states with his stuff.

Now he needed a diversion, some way to draw Kellerman's fire, if it came to that. He shifted his gaze to the mannequins he used for target practice. The Yankee fan with the ball cap was the least damaged. He threw it over his shoulder like a dead guy and juggled everything all the way up the stairs.

The bartender raised his brows. "What are you going to do with that?"

"Catch me a rat."

Outside, he opened the Mercedes' trunk and set his defenses inside. After one long look at his club and its dark marquee, he hoped he'd see it again, got in behind the wheel, and peeled out onto the highway toward his luxury apartment in a gated community, which gave him little comfort considering the veracity and brutality of his enemy.

***

Jesse dashed into the hospital and sprinted up the stairs to ICU. At the nurses' station, he stopped, out of breath. "Open the door...I want to see my sister."

"Slow down, young man," the duty nurse said. "I don't want you running in there like a madman. She's awake, but she's by no means ready for any excitement."

"Okay. I get it. I'll be cool. It'll be so good to hear her voice again."

"Ah...about that. She can't speak yet on account of one particularly nasty knife wound and the ventilator tube, so you won't be hearing much more than her coughing and grunting."

It's worse than I thought. "Thanks for the warning."

The nurse hit the button to open the door.

Jesse walked in, calm as could be, but inside he was screaming with joy. Behind curtain number two, he found his mom and Uncle Francis. He strode directly to Clarissa's bedside and took stock of her situation. She stared at him as if he were the devil

~163~

himself, the fear on her face unnerving. "What's wrong with her?"

"We don't know," Jude said. "She's been like this since Kellerman was here—"

"No way. He was here?" Jesse bent to her. "What did he say?"

She shook her head no.

"No? Nothing?"

Only a grunting, raspy sound came from her throat. Then she did the strangest thing, pointed to her pillow with her three-fingered bandaged hand.

"The pillow? He took your pillow."

She nodded and placed both bandaged hands on her face.

"Son of a bitch." That could only mean one thing. He came here to kill her...smother her... no blood, no bruised throat... He grabbed the nurse call button from the sheet and pressed it frantically, over and over.

"Jesse," Jude cried. "What are you thinking?"

A nurse rushed in. "What's the matter?"

Jesse dropped the button. "Get security in here to keep Kellerman out. He tried to kill her."

The nurse frowned. "No he didn't. He was a perfect gentleman."

"Bull. He was going to smother her with the

pillow."

"The pillow? Don't be silly. He was fluffing it up for her."

"Look at her. She's scared shitless. Fluff my ass." He grabbed his mom's shoulders and looked straight into her shock-widened eyes. "Don't leave her side..." a glance at Uncle Francis, "Both of you stay with her. He'll be back, I guarantee it. And he's a tricky son of a bitch. Don't fall for any of his nice-guy crap. Keep him away from her."

"Why would he try to kill her?" Jude asked.

Francis scowled. "Yeah. He's trying to solve the case."

"Because he's the guy who did this to her."

The two exchanged shocked glances.

A message from Nick Fortune buzzed in on the phone. *'Something's come up. I need you to come in early, cover for me. Busy night...'* Yada yada.

Shit.

"What's going on, Jesse?" Jude cried.

"I don't have time to explain it. Nurse, get security now. I've got to go...to find Nick Fortune. Kellerman's on the war path...nobody is safe." He patted Clarissa's arm. "Don't worry, sis. I've got your back."

Jim Keane

Chapter Sixteen

The Bliss was a madhouse. The allure of half-price drinks for the ladies drew in the men, as well, looking to get lucky. The line stretched from the door and back into the parking lot. The bouncers couldn't check IDs fast enough.

Jesse pressed through the crowd to get inside. Hip-Hop music rattled the walls and patrons filled the dance floor, a rocking night to be sure. He worked his way to the bar, and not seeing Fortune, asked the bartender, "Where is Nick?"

He didn't even look up while pouring a line of Jägermeister shots. "Out."

"Doing what?"

"Rat hunting's what he said."

"What's that supposed to mean?"

He placed the glasses on a tray. "Can't you see I'm slammed?"

The music stopped. Moans and curses rose from the crowd.

Jesse glanced to the DJ booth. A Peekskill patrol officer stood there holding the plug of an electrical cord.

"Listen up, everybody." This came from an officer at the door. He and a partner held the bouncer between them, by his arms. "Where's the owner?"

Jesse remained mute, mostly out of defiance. Nobody else said anything.

"We can do this the easy way or the hard way." Two more cops stepped in behind him. "I'll ask one more time. Where is Nick Fortune?"

"He isn't here," barmaid Ginger said, the feisty redhead that she was. "Who do you think you are, Mad Max, kicking ass and taking names?"

The cop stepped forward. "You some kind of smart ass? Answer my question. Where is he?"

"We haven't seen him."

The cop stationed at the DJ booth started bulling toward her with a billy club raised. The crowd backed away from her.

Jesse couldn't let her take a hit for Fortune. He pressed past patrons and stopped in the bully cop's path. "No need for violence, you guys. What's this all about?"

"We got a report of underage drinking in this pothole." Mad Max waved a piece of paper. "Search warrant."

"Search all you want," Jesse said. "He's not

here."

The cop with the warrant strode to Jesse. "Who the hell are you, the manager or something?"

"Jesse Curley. I'm covering for Mr. Fortune tonight."

"I know that name. Curley. You're the perp who cold-cocked Kellerman." He balled his fists. "You want to go a round with me, boy?"

A stout man wearing a green Irish tweed cap stepped from the crowd, rolling up his sleeves. "I just may take you up on that, bobbie."

"Who the hell are you?"

"Name's O'Rourke. Rory O'Rourke. You come here lookin' for trouble? I say ye found yourself plenty."

"Is everyone around here a smart ass?" The cop crooked his neck and spoke into a shoulder mic. "Dispatch. Tell Kellerman his suspect isn't here."

"Roger."

Suspect? Sure enough. Kellerman was going to pin the assault on Fortune.

"We're done here, boys." He turned to the door. "Carry on, you numb nuts." He rotated his hand above his head like he was twirling a lasso to round up his troops.

The DJ spun a disc and restarted the music, but

the patrons just milled about as if they were no longer in a party mood.

Ginger nuzzled up to Jesse. "Thanks for what you did back there. I thought for sure that cop was going to club me."

"They were fishing. I doubt that paper was even a signed search warrant."

She rushed off to hustle drinks.

Rory approached Jesse, sleeves still rolled up. "Fishing, ya say?"

"They got nothing on Fortune. He didn't attack my sister."

"The lass who got knifed in the alley?" His Irish accent was thick as mud.

"Yeah. Kellerman is fishing for suspects."

"I tried to help 'er. Done what I could."

"Oh. That was you? I heard about a good Samaritan. I'm Jesse."

"Don't know a thing about Samaritans, but I'm glad to meetcha, laddy."

"You saved her life, you know."

"Sure do, but that Kellerman fella tried to blame me for the attack, the arsehole."

"Now Fortune is in the detective's crosshairs."

No doubt he had the flash drive with him, the evidence against Kellerman. If the dirty cop got his hands on it, he'd surely destroy it.

I have to break into that security computer downstairs, make another copy.

"Thanks for your help, Rory. Hey, do you mind hanging out? I got something I gotta do."

"Go ahead. I'll watch ye back, Jesse."

He ducked behind the bar, through the door, and down the stairs, and got the shock of the day. The computer was unlocked. *Why? Unless... Fortune gave me access to the videos in case whatever he was up to went south.* Jesse sat at the monitor, found a flash drive in the top drawer, and started copying files.

***

Meanwhile, at the Peekskill Police Department, Kellerman prepared his Glock and loaded five extra clips to carry in his jacket. He knew Nick Fortune had a gun and wasn't afraid to use it. That would be a grave mistake on his part.

Kellerman's blood flowed hot, his nerves on fire, the way he always felt before a big bust. He had enough circumstantial evidence on Fortune to pin him with a bad rap, but a confession would put the nail in his coffin. Extracting confessions, false or otherwise, was his specialty. Hours and hours under a bright light made a man sweat and say anything necessary to get out of an interrogation room.

Fortune had come to the station with the flash drive he'd requested, but there must've been a video on it he hadn't seen, something that Fortune wanted only the captain to see. It was no doubt incriminating, so Kellerman had told the Duty Sergeant that Fortune had come to confess but got cold feet, squashing any doubt amongst his peers that he was a solid suspect in the attack on Clarissa Curley.

The mission to bring Nick Fortune in for questioning would hopefully go bad, resulting in the justified use of deadly force, and then he could get on with his goal of revenge for his daughter, confined to a wheelchair, a little girl rotting away in a body that perpetually lingered near death.

He exited the station, loaded and ready...but of all the bad luck, he ran into Officer Keith Clarkson.

"Hey, detective. What's going on?"

"None of your business." He attempted to step around Keith, but the tenacious officer blocked him. *Do I have to shoot him right here, on the sidewalk in front of headquarters?* "You don't want to interfere with an official police investigation."

"I heard Nick Fortune came in to confess."

"You heard right," Kellerman snarled. "Now get out of my way."

"But why didn't he want to talk to you?"

"How should I know? He turned chickenshit and ran off."

"If I were you, I'd head out to bring him in."

Kellerman closed his right hand into a fist. "What do you want, man?"

"I want in on the bust, make sure it goes down nice and legal like."

"You think I don't know what I'm doing?"

"Fortune is no pushover. You know it. I know it. He's a hardened combat vet. You'll need me to cover your ass."

"If you're done brownnosing, move. I've got a job to do."

"You be careful, you hear." Keith stepped aside.

Fucker. Kellerman pushed by him, stalked around the corner to the POLICE VEHICLES ONLY parking lot, and jumped into his Tahoe. He appreciated how eager the young officer wanted to get in on the action...reminded him of himself not long ago. After graduating from the academy, he was much the same way. While on foot patrol in the South Bronx, where the crackle of gunfire happened more than the ringing of the public school bell, he would climb up to the rooftops with binoculars, scanning for potential drug dealers and streetwalkers plying their trade. Officer Harry Kellerman was a secret agent on a clandestine mission to rid the city of its criminals, ducking low, peeking into alleys, hiding in the bushes, ever vigilant. Oh yeah, he was a big deal back then, until his daughter got crippled by a cop's stray bullet.

Having worked himself into a rage, he started the engine and peeled out onto eastbound Central Ave, code 3. Since the squad he'd sent to the Bliss came up empty-handed, he'd searched Motor Vehicle Department records for Fortune's Mercedes, came up with his residential address, barely over a mile from the police station. Kellerman's gut instinct told him he'd be there.

***

Keith stood in front of the police station and watched the black Tahoe speed away, back window lights flashing. Something about Kellerman didn't pass the smell test. Why would he insist on facing Fortune alone? Had NYPD turned him into a one-man wrecking crew, or was he about to do something he didn't want his fellow officers to witness?

Besides, any notion that Nick Fortune had attacked Clarissa seemed well beyond the realm of reality. Keith had known the club owner for many years. Yeah, Fortune was tough but not stupid enough to attack one of his patrons, a woman no less, outside his club. The smell test became a stink bomb. Kellerman was out to get the wrong man. But why?

I'm going to find out what that detective is up to.

He jumped into his marked squad car, flipped on the overheads, and raced off in the direction Kellerman had gone. The bobblehead cop on the dash waggled to beat the band. As he weaved through traffic, he recalled how police officers relied on their training and instincts to pursue leads and solve puzzles. *Observe, listen, and question everything you see and hear. Be proactive, not reactive.* In this case, he had to adhere to that sage advice from the instructors at the academy.

Keith Clarkson didn't become a cop to write parking tickets in a small town. His calling entailed tracking leads and hunting criminals. *To serve and protect.* Watching from the bench wasn't in his DNA. Even if this mad chase after Kellerman led to nothing, he was in the thick of the action, right where he was meant to be.

He chirped the siren through a red light. Kellerman's Tahoe was speeding a quarter mile ahead of him. The hunt was on.

Chapter Seventeen

Kellerman arrived at Hudson Valley Condominiums, an exclusive community with a clubhouse, two tennis courts, and an Olympic-sized pool. He smashed through the gate and raced past a jitney stand that supplied transport service to the Metro North rail station. Bloated grey clouds lumbered across the sky while a kettle of turkey vultures circled above. He killed the lights and siren, and careened onto the tree-lined drive toward the multiplex of apartment blocks with beveled roofs, the largest standing four stories high and sporting an odd spire, most likely a decorative cell tower.

He cruised the parking lots around the complex, looking for the Mercedes Fortune owned. Excitement of the impending bust manifested itself in a raised heartbeat and a moistening of his brow. In back, there it was, shielded behind a stand of trees.

Fortune is here, alright. "You can't hide from me..." Or maybe that wasn't his play. Fortune was not one to hide...

Kellerman claimed two parking spots at the front

entrance then double-checked his Glock and the five clips in two pockets of his jacket. He expected a gunfight, as he was sure Fortune would not be happy to see him at his door. On that, Kellerman was counting. He got out and made his way up the shady walk to the portico, where residents sat around in patio chairs, socializing until he stepped up.

"You new here?" one resident asked. Another put in, "Never seen you here before." A particularly observant guy said, "You a cop?" A nice lady asked, "Is something going down we should know about?"

He displayed his badge. "There's no problem, ma'am. I'm Detective Kellerman. A routine investigation, is all. You can go about your business." When he yanked on the door handle, he discovered it was locked. *Damn keyless security.* A bit embarrassed he turned back to the tenants. "Anybody want to buzz me in?"

The nice lady stepped up, swiped a keycard across the door sensor, and the lock released with a click.

"Thank you, ma'am."

"Always obliged to help the police."

He stepped inside. The first thing he noticed was the crisp cool air and the scent of flowers. Hotel quality carpet with a diamond design gave the hallways, to the left and to the right, a ritzy accent, as did the sconces, mirrors, and Greek paintings on the walls. An elevator stood before him; a gaggle of tenants awaited its arrival, and a door marked STAIRCASE was offset on the right. Rather than fight a crowd in the elevator, he skulked up the stairs to the fourth floor, and traversing a similar hallway as downstairs, he heard Jazz music emanating from somewhere, trumpets and coronets with a heady bass beat, and when he found door Number 412, a penthouse suit, oddly, the door stood slightly ajar. A TV blared from inside, applause then *"Entertainment for 100...and the answer is Mickey Mouse..."*

He drew his gun. Perhaps the club owner had gone to the laundry room, or stepped out momentarily to get some ice. Whatever the case, why would Fortune be so careless as to leave his door open for any reason? *Or maybe this is an ambush.* He heard the elevator ding a few doors down. *Fortune coming back? B*ut a quick glance revealed Officer Keith Clarkson stepping out. *What the fuck?*

Gun drawn, he stalked forward. "Hey there, detective—"

"Shhhh. You shouldn't be here," Kellerman whispered as blood boiled in his veins.

"At least now you won't have to call for

backup." He glanced at the open door. "Where's Fortune?"

"Get on the opposite side of the door and shut up."

In position, Keith nodded.

Politics for 50...and the answer is the wigs...

Kellerman pressed his shoulder against the doorframe, Glock held pointed up, and he pushed the door fully open. TV applause got louder. He peeked inside. Beyond a short foyer and into the living room, the back of a couch faced him, the TV blasting from across the room, a flat-screen mounted to the wall. Fortune, wearing a baseball cap, sat on the couch, facing the TV, his back to the long arm of the law. This confrontation would be easier without Clarkson looking over his shoulder. He'd have to play it by the book.

"Fortune," Kellerman shouted. "Peekskill Police. I want to ask you a couple of questions."

Fortune didn't move.

Keith teetered sideways to get a look for himself. "Isn't it obvious he's sleeping?" He brushed past Kellerman...

"No, wait."

"Relax. He's a friend of mine." He strode into the suite like he owned the place.

History for 20...and the answer is Napoleon...

"Mr. Fortune, Wake up. We just want to talk."

Gunfire erupted. Bullets pocked the right foyer wall.

"Get down," Kellerman yelled.

Clarkson keeled over.

Kellerman nosedived to the floor and trained his gun on the living room. "Fortune. You just killed a cop. Drop your weapon and come out with your hands up."

"Fuck you, Kellerman. I know what you did, and I have proof."

"Yeah...I was afraid you would. Now I have to kill you."

"Good luck with that." Fortune bounded across the living room, a blur of a man, firing his weapon into the foyer. Bullets pulverized the hallway walls, exploding two sconce lamps and a mirror with a ritzy frame.

Kellerman kept his head down and took cover behind the doorframe. The gun blasts made his ears ring, and the acrid smell of cordite filled his nostrils with the sweet smell of battle. He returned fire, striking the figure on the couch. The baseball cap went flying, and the head exploded into dusty fragments.

What kind of happy shit is this?

He saw Clarkson crawling toward the door. His Kevlar vest must've saved him.

"Automobiles for 100...and the answer is..."

Fortune made another run across the living room, blasting away. A bullet struck Clarkson's leg. He screamed. Kellerman supplied cover fire, shattering the TV into silence, while Clarkson dragged himself clear of the foyer and into the hallway. Blood was a geyser coming from the leg wound. Kellerman lugged Clarkson to cover behind the wall, then he pressed his left hand against the wound, hoping to stem the squirt from a ruptured femoral artery.

"What a cluster-fuck. This is why I work alone."

"I smell cookies," Keith said with a smile. "Chocolate chip cookies."

He was going into shock.

Kellerman reached for the radio mic on Keith's shoulder, but before he could call for medical, Fortune opened fire again, this time from the foyer and moving forward. He wore a beret cocked on his head, bandoleers across his chest, and full Desert Storm body armor. Bullets cracked through the air and into the hallway. Greek gods and nymphs were torn to shreds.

Kellerman hauled Keith toward the stairwell with his left hand while he fired at the open doorway with his right, hoping Fortune would stick his head out and get it blown off.

By the time Kellerman breached the door to the stairs, Keith's lips were turning blue. Kellerman yanked off his belt and wrapped it around Keith's bleeding leg. "I told you this is none of your business."

Though his eyes were open wide, he didn't respond.

Kellerman pulled the belt as tight as he could and double-looped it in place.

Fortune leaped into the hallway, firing like a madman. Bullets tore into the stairwell door.

Kellerman propped it open a crack and fired back. Three shots hit dead center mass, driving Fortune back into his suite.

"Don't go anywhere," he told Keith and bounded after Fortune. He got to the door just in time to see him lean against the bullet-riddled couch and pull the pin on a grenade. "Drop it."

Fortune smiled.

"No, don't drop it."

He tossed the grenade. Kellerman shot him in the face, sending him back over the couch. The grenade bounced into the hallway and did a little pirouette at Kellerman's feet. "No shit." He took off toward the stairwell. A blinding flash shook the walls, and a wave of scorching heat and eardrum-splitting thunder knocked him to the floor. The pressure was a sledgehammer to the skull, and his back was on fire: piercing pain, a lot of piercing pain.

Fire alarms blared.

The ceiling came down.

Darkness swallowed him.

Chapter Eighteen

J esse organized the video clips on the security computer hard drive into a file of powerful evidence against Kellerman, and while the files were being copied to a flash drive, he called Fortune's cell phone. He needed to know the cops had been here looking for him. It rang and rang and rang, then jumped to voicemail. *"You've reached the phone of Nick Fortune. If your call is important, leave a message. If not, fuck off."*

"Shit." He hung up.

File transfer 48%.

He dialed his mom.

She answered. "Jesse, are you okay?"

"Has Kellerman shown up there?"

"No, thank God. Clarissa is sleeping peacefully. Francis went down to the cafeteria for coffee."

"You're there all by yourself? Mom—"

"They've posted two guards at the nurses' station. It's been pretty quiet. What are you doing? When will you be back?"

"Don't let your guard down. I have to find my

boss. Gotta run."

"Bye."

He hung up.

File transfer 100%.

He pulled the drive from the USB port, put it in his pocket with the cell phone, and bounded up the stairs. Business was back to the usual dancing and drinking.

Rory was seated at the bar. "You good?"

"Done." Jesse looked at the bartender. "Nick's in trouble. He's not answering his phone. I've got to find him...at his apartment maybe."

"We've got this handled here, Jess," the bartender replied. "Go."

Rory stood. "I'm going with you."

"Great. My car is a piece of shit, won't start half the time. You can drive."

***

Kellerman's view of his surroundings came to light, as hazy as trudging through fog. His head throbbed, and his back seared with white-hot pain. A clamorous ringing echoed in his ears. Choking smoke burned his nostrils. He coughed.

A distant voice spoke. "Take it easy. We got you."

His blurred vision focused on a police officer and

an EMT. They were wheeling him somewhere on a gurney, a bumpy ride. He could see the sky was overcast with gray clouds...no, it was smoke...smoke was billowing from the building. Fire licked from the upper windows. Fortune had made a mess of his last stand.

The gurney weaved between rattling fire trucks parked helter-skelter. Hoses, fat with water pressure, twisted and turned every which way, and the air was alive with the sounds of sirens and screams. Open doors of an ambulance appeared. He was lifted up, and with a clank and a joggle, he was shoved inside. A blonde EMT slapped an oxygen mask on his face.

"Wait..." He coughed.

"Don't speak," she said. "You'll be alright."

"Damn it." He pulled the mask down. "Officer Clarkson—"

"Relax." She forced the mask back over his face.

"Is he alive?" His voice came out raspy and muffled.

"You're on the way to the hospital."

"He was bleeding pretty bad."

"Quiet, you're lucky to be alive."

Doors slammed shut and the ambulance lunged into motion, siren wailing.

***

Fire belched plumes of smoke that spiraled into the air. Windows exploded. Sirens blared. A crowd of onlookers gathered behind yellow crime scene tape strung from tree to tree. Police stood guard, and firefighters rushed in and out of the building. Chaos and destruction had come to Hudson Valley Condos.

Jesse, riding shotgun, couldn't believe what he was seeing.

Rory jammed on the brakes, the tires screeching as the cab stopped in the apartment complex's east parking lot. He rubbed the back of his neck and surveyed the mayhem. "Jaysus."

Jesse bailed out and ran a beeline to a cop holding bystanders back. "What happened?"

"Some kind of explosion. You live here?"

"No, but—"

"Then get the hell out of here. None of this is your concern."

Jesse surveyed the scene, spotted Kellerman's black Tahoe parked in the front lot...and a police cruiser next to it, but nowhere near the other responding officers' cars. Even from here, he could see the bobblehead cop on the dashboard.

Rory caught up with Jesse. "What's the scoop?"

"That's Keith's cruiser, my friend on the force. He could help us find out if Fortune is here, but I don't see him anywhere."

"Maybe he's inside the building."

Jesse asked the cop, "Do you know where I can find Officer Clarkson?"

"What don't you understand about get the hell out of here?"

Jesse stepped back and called Keith's cell phone. It rang and rang and rang. He didn't wait for voicemail. "He isn't answering."

"He could be a mite busy."

A coroner's van backed up to the front entrance. Two guys in gray jumpsuits got out, opened the rear doors, rolled out a gurney, and wheeled it inside. "Look." Jesse pointed. "They're here for a body. Somebody got killed in there."

"Lordy. What's happened to this small town? Used to be jaywalking was the most likely way to get killed."

With hope on a string, Jesse redialed Fortune's number.

No answer.

"Damn. And where the hell is Kellerman?"

A lady stepped from the crowd. "Are you looking for that detective?"

Jesse nodded. "I'd like to know where he is." *So I know he's not killing my sister.*

"I helped him get inside. A true gentleman he was. Then we heard a lot of gunfire and an explosion."

"Aye," Rory said. "He must'a found Mr. Fortune."

"The firemen got here quick, and the cops, and before long, an ambulance came and took an injured man away. I don't know who it was, though, but I haven't seen the detective since."

A half dozen cops exited the building and held up several sheets to block the view from bystanders and reporters. Through a gap in the barrier, Jesse saw a black body bag on the gurney pass by. The coroner's van joggled, the rear doors closed, and the van sped away. The cops gathered the sheets together and somberly strode back inside.

"Come on, Rory. Let's go."

"Where to, laddy?"

"The hospital to find out who was in that ambulance." Jesse nodded to the nice lady. "Thanks for your help."

"Always obliged."

At a full run, he followed Rory to the cab, and they were off to Hudson Valley E-R.

***

As Kellerman awoke, bright lights filled his

vision. *Am I dead?* He was ready to face his judgment day. Would saints and angels welcome him to Heaven with trumpets and harps, or would devils and demons welcome him with fire and smoke, all licking their chops in the Ninth Circle of Hell? Whichever fate awaited him, so be it, as everything he'd done wrong was for the love of his daughter.

A nurse stood above him. "He's coming out of it."

"Where am I?"

"Hudson Valley Recovery."

He glanced around, saw a gray curtain, heard noisy machines, tried to get up, but extreme vertigo forced him back down. "What the hell happened?"

"You just came out of surgery."

"Surgery?"

"Your back. Don't you remember?"

"What's wrong with my back?"

The nurse gripped his shoulder. "Shrapnel from that grenade turned it to hamburger."

"Grenade?" He looked down to see his torso wrapped in white bandages, realized his head was wrapped the same way. "Was I in a war?"

"From what I hear, yes."

"Yes?"

"It took the doctors three hours to pluck out all

the metal fragments and wood splinters from your back."

"It's all a blur."

"You've got a nasty concussion, too. It'll all come back to you once the anesthesia wears off. Best thing you can do now is sleep it off."

I don't even remember my name.

***

Jesse held on as Rory careened the cab into the hospital's chaotic EMERGENCY entrance where double-parked police cruisers and ambulances jammed the portico. He had to talk to whoever came here from the Hudson Valley Condos fire. Rory parked between two ambulances and Jesse jumped out. Automatic doors slid open as he hurried inside. The emergency waiting room was packed: people with broken bones and burns...and a dozen cops, at least. He didn't see Officer Clarkson nor Detective Kellerman among them.

Jesse flagged down a nurse. "I need to see the man they brought here from the condo fire."

She waved a hand to the chattering crowd. "You're looking at them."

"All of them?" His heart pounded. "Have you admitted Officer Keith Clarkson?"

The nurse's cheeks reddened. "Not that I know

of. You should go home and call later for updates."
She clapped her hands and whistled like a sailor.
"Listen up, people. We can't allow any more people
in here. If you're not injured, go outside and wait."

"Wait for what?" Jesse asked.

"One of their own went down."

"Who?"

"I don't have that information, now will you
please go."

"All right. We're going."

Jesse led Rory outside to the parking lot, where a
familiar and unsavory cop, Mad Max, stopped them.
"Well, if it ain't the numb-nuts from the Bliss. What
are you doing here?"

"There's an officer down. Do you know who?"

"Not yet. We're waiting for word."

Rory shrugged. "Tis a mystery."

"Don't you two have anything better to do?"

"He's no help. Come on, Rory. While we're here,
you should meet my sister." Jesse led him around the
corner to the front entrance, where there was no
chaotic crowd. On the elevator ride up to the ICU,
Rory seemed nervous. "It's alright. She doesn't bite."

"I don't know, laddy. Last time I saw her, she
was in a bad way. What do I say to her?"

"Just don't tell her any bad Irish jokes."

He laughed. The door dinged open. Down the hallway, two hospital security guards flanked the double doors. They wore charcoal gray uniforms, sported gold badges and caps with HVHS letters on the front panel. Kellerman couldn't pull rank on them because Hudson Valley Hospital Security personnel were not under the jurisdiction of the Peekskill Police Department.

"Why the guards?" Rory asked.

"To keep Kellerman out."

"What is it you haven't told me?"

Jesse pulled him into the waiting area. "The guy you saw in the alley...that was Kellerman."

"Could have been, I guess. He's big enough."

Jesse pulled the flash drive from his pocket. "It's all here." He held it up for Rory's inspection. "On video."

"But, laddy. Why would he attack your sister?"

"And that's the million-dollar question, my man."

"I want to see the video for me self."

"After you meet my sister." He pocketed the flash drive and led Rory to the nurses' station.

"Mr. Curley." The duty nurse pressed the button. "Go right in."

At the open doors, he stopped to address the

guard on the right. "Thanks for keeping my sister safe." He swept his gaze to the guard on the left. "Both of you."

They nodded.

He walked in and led Rory to curtain number two. Peeking in first, he saw his mom and uncle on duty, sitting in bedside chairs. Styrofoam cups were stacked on the side table. Clarissa's bed was cranked up, but she was still bandaged pretty much everywhere.

Jesse stepped in. "Hi, Mom."

She jumped up. "Jesse. Don't sneak up on us like that. We're on pins and needles as it is."

"Sorry." He nodded to Francis. "This is Rory O'Rourke."

He tipped his head to the two then moved to Clarissa's bedside. "Lass...and how are you feelin'?"

She looked at him with a questioning crook on her brow.

"Oh," Jesse said. "I forgot to tell you. She can't speak yet. Clarissa, this man saved your life, stemmed some of the bleeding until the EMTs got there."

"Weren't that heroic a deed, ma'am. Happy to be of help."

She reached out with a bandaged hand and mouthed, "Thank you."

"Just get better quick, okay?"

Jude touched Jesse's arm. "Did you find your boss?"

"He's MIA, and Kellerman, too, so you have to stay sharp."

"Are you leaving again?"

"Sorry, Mom. We're going back to the Bliss, take care of business while Fortune is gone." *And watch the video again.*

"Nice meeting you all." Rory waved.

Before long, they were back in the cab, racing at breakneck speed past slower traffic to the outskirts of Peekskill.

The Bliss was rocking. Jesse checked with the bartender. He looked frazzled, juggling drinks and drafts. "We need ice up here, and I'm down to two bottles of light beer." He had to shout over the loud music. It was a wonder he wasn't completely deaf by now.

"We've got to give him a hand, Rory. Are you up to some back-breaking work?"

"Whatever you need, laddy."

Jesse led the way downstairs. "Beer cases are in the cooler. I'll get the ice."

Rory stopped at the bank of monitors, all in sleep mode, screensavers waving and curling. "Pretty fancy."

"Once we get caught up, I'll show you the video. In particular, the clip that captured what Kellerman did when he returned to the alley as the detective in charge of the investigation."

"Must be compelling."

"It's downright damning."

After the ice was delivered and the beer bins were restocked, déjà vu struck Jesse all over again. The music stopped. The ceiling lights blazed on, and the dancers groaned. "Hey." "What the hell?" "Are you fuckin' kidding me?"

"Peekskill Police. Everybody freeze."

Jesse fought to hold back his temper and stepped into the aisle to face off with that same bully cop, Mad Max. "What can I do for you, officer?"

"Search warrant."

"Yeah. That's what you said last time."

"Forever the smart ass, huh, Curley. Everybody up against the wall." He pointed to the dance floor's back wall, mirrored and plastered with neon beer signs. Most patrons obeyed, some remained at the bar. Others bolted out the back door. Mad Max didn't give them a second look. Ginger and Sylvia stood at the barmaid stand, looking perturbed at yet another interruption in their tip streams.

Mad Max tromped up to Jesse and shoved an official-looking document at him. "Computers. Where are they? And I mean all of them, or me and boys will tear this place apart."

No. No. No. That could only mean one thing. Kellerman got Fortune, got the flash drive, and now he wants the source files. Without them, there'd be no way to prove a case against him. *The bad guy wins again. Kellerman and Conrad should start a club.*

By now, the bartender joined Jesse and Rory in front of Mad Max. "Give him what he wants, Jesse, so we can get back to the business at hand. All this cops and robbers bullshit is above our pay grade."

Shit. If the cops take the security computer, that leaves only the flash drive in my pocket. Don't do anything that will warrant getting frisked. Jesse glanced at Rory.

He shrugged.

"The security computer. That's what Kellerman wants, right?"

"It's evidence in my investigation." This came from the bass voice of a bald, gray-suited gentleman at the door. He wore a badge on a lanyard around his neck.

"Who are you?" Jesse asked.

"Detective Doherty. It's my investigation now. And believe me, I'm not happy about being called back from vacation early. So your full cooperation will be much appreciated."

So it was Kellerman in that body bag.

The revelation was shocking, and for his sister's sake, a relief at the same time. Maybe now the video will fall into the hands of someone who can put the blame where it belonged and get Fortune off the hook.

"It's downstairs." Jesse pointed to the door behind the bar. "Through there."

Mad Max led a few of his men to loot the basement.

Detective Doherty shouted, "Everyone must leave the premises now. We're shutting it down."

Jesse couldn't believe it. "Come on, man. We work here."

"Not anymore, you don't. The owner of this establishment is deceased."

"Fortune? Dead?" *What is happening?*

"We have orders to clear you all out of here as a public nuisance. And Jesse Curley, you're coming with me to the station."

"Why?"

"I have a few questions for you."

"You're putting me through that bullshit again?"

"Are you coming easy, or should I slap on the

cuffs."

Shit. They'll frisk me and find the flash drive.

Jesse realized Rory would never get a chance to see the video proof of Kellerman's treachery...unless... He slipped the flash drive from his pocket and nudged Rory's arm. The handoff was as slick as any drug dealer could pull off.

"Cuffs it is then."

Jesse threw up his hands. "I'm coming. No trouble." As he walked toward the detective, his heart thumped with dread and uncertainty, not knowing what could go wrong next.

The shit keeps hitting the fan.

Chapter Nineteen

Kellerman awoke from the deepest sleep he could remember. That anesthetic was a doozy. An IV bag dripped fluids into his arm, and a heart monitor beeped. He appeared to be in a private room, TV on the wall, door to his personal toilet. His memory no longer failed him, the gunfight in Fortune's suit, the grenade. It had all come back. The son of a bitch had set a trap for him. *His actions further cements my contention that he was guilty of the assault on Carissa Curley.* Case Closed. Now there remained only one person who could point the finger at him, *and she isn't long for this world.*

"Mr. Kellerman. Good to see you coming around."

"I feel lightheaded."

"That's normal. You have a visitor."

"I need to get out of here."

She patted his shoulder. "You're not going anywhere." She turned to the door. "I told him you need rest, but he's insistent. Says he's your boss."

Kellerman peered at a tall man with white hair

and a vein-reddened nose, standing at the door. He wore captain bars on his collar and a gruff expression.

Now came the blame game. *What the hell went wrong*, he'd ask, because nothing had gone as planned. He'd appoint a review board, initiate an internal investigation, a shoot team would be on him like buffalo shit on the prairie. Nick Fortune was his suspect. He assaulted a police officer, resisted arrest, and became a one-man strike force. Even though the shooting was justified, police bureaucracy would run him through the wringer.

The captain stepped into the room.

"Just a couple of minutes," the nurse said and walked out.

Kellerman groaned. "Captain."

"How are you feeling?"

"Too soon to tell."

"Don't mind if I stand. This won't take long."

Kellerman winced. "What's on your mind."

"Seems your investigation has run off the rails, Lieutenant." He stabbed an accusatory finger at him. "A police officer is dead, and a respected citizen as well."

"Fortune? Respected. I had him dead to rights on aggravated assault. He damn near killed that girl. I was there to bring him in for questioning. I didn't know he'd go all Rambo on me and Officer Clarkson."

The captain's eyebrows shot up. "Nick Fortune is a suspect?"

"He came in to confess but chickened out. I had to run him down."

"So you go in guns blazing?"

"He fired at us. I damn near got Clarkson out of the line of fire...until Fortune came at us, firing as if he had no fear of death. I plugged him once though, sent him back inside long enough to get Clarkson to safety in the stairwell. But he was bleeding pretty bad. I had to end the threat to save him. I went back in to re-engage. Who'd have thought Fortune had a grenade up his sleeve."

"I've given you a lot of leeway since you came to our small town. A big-shot detective from the NYPD. You went off half-cocked without filing a single report on what you were doing to solve the case. What did they teach you in the city?"

"How to stay alive."

"You leave me no choice but to take you off the Curley investigation."

"You can't do that. It's my case."

"I just did. Doherty is in charge now. When you're up and out of here, report to my office."

The captain turned for the door.

"I was doing my job, sir. Fortune turned it into a cluster-fuck."

He stopped and turned around. "We'll let CSI and Internal Affairs make that call. Officially, you're on medical leave." And he walked out.

"It's not my fault."

The nurse returned. "Settle down. You wanna bust your stitches?"

"I've got to get out of here."

"I know. Everybody wants to get outta here." She untangled the IV tube. "Get some rest. Doctor's orders."

Fuck!

***

Jesse paced the police station's interrogation room, his thoughts racing. *I can't believe I'm back here again.* At the rate he was racking up charges, he'd be doing a stint in Sing Sing, for sure. *Hardened criminal. Convict number 123456.*

He plopped into one of three folding chairs and slammed his fist on the table. With any luck, which he didn't have according to Conrad, this new detective would be more reasonable than Kellerman. *Yeah, that's it. Think positive.* He scoped out the mirror on the wall, no doubt a two-way job. The detective could have watched him throw that fit. He scanned the high corners, spotted two cameras and found some solace that video in this room would tell the true story of what would come down between him and Doherty. There'd be no trumped-up charges for assault on a police officer.

But what was next? A bogus rap for the explosion at Fortune's apartment? Maybe aiding and abetting the criminal who had assaulted his sister. Where would the police corruption end? Nick Fortune wouldn't stand for being framed, fought back, got killed in the process, but he took Kellerman with him. *Ah, the proverbial silver lining?*

The door opened, and Doherty walked in, his tanned bald head aglow under the ceiling lights. He dropped a ream of paper on the table. "So you're the notorious Jesse Curley I've read so much about." He pointed to the papers. "Attempted bank robbery, assault on a police officer, all in a week. Before that, the Motor Vehicle Department has the only record that you even existed." He sat across from Jesse. "What the hell is wrong with you?"

"Kellerman was out to get me. I don't know why me, or why he attacked my sister, but something wasn't right with that guy. He was a dirty cop, I tell you. Got what he deserved."

Doherty leaned back in his chair, mouth agape as if stunned yet processing this new information.

Jesse kept it coming. "You've got the security computer from the Bliss. Take a good look at every angle inside the club. You won't learn anything from the actual assault clips. It's afterwards, when Kellerman walks the crime scene. You'll see it, and you'll know what I'm talking about."

"Interesting." Doherty leaned forward. "How did you get access to that computer? My lab boys tell me it's voice locked."

Shit. They had to unplug it to take it. A reboot would initiate its security protocols. With Fortune being dead, they'll never see that video. "Nick showed it to me. He had it on a flash drive, probably in his pocket. The coroner should find it."

"That's not going to happen. His body was burned to a crisp in the fire, not a thread of clothes left on him. Any flash drive would be ashes, as well."

That image soured his stomach. "No. No. Don't tell me—"

"I'm afraid it's your word against his."

"Huh? What word? He's dead."

Doherty stared at him as if what he heard was incomprehensible.

"He's dead, right?"

"Somehow you got your wires crossed. Detective Kellerman is alive...in the hospital, but alive."

"What hospital?"

"Hudson Valley—"

Shock made Jesse's next breath a gasp. "No. No. No. My sister's in that hospital. He tried to kill her once. He's going to try again. You've got to do something—"

"Whoa, whoa, whoa, slow down, boy."

Jesse shot out of his chair. "If you won't do something, I will." He bounded five steps to the door, yanked on the handle... It didn't budge. Locked. "Son of a bitch, let me out of here."

"Sit down, Mr. Curley, or I'll put you in chains."

"No. You don't understand...wait." Jesse sat down and leaned toward Doherty. "They said a cop and a citizen were killed..." He remembered seeing Keith's car at the scene. "If not Kellerman...what cop got killed?"

He glanced at the mirror and shrugged. "That information hasn't been released. I can't say."

"Don't give me any of that happy horseshit about next-of-kin notifications. Was it Keith Clarkson?"

"Why would you think that?"

"Because his squad car was there, at the scene of

the fire. I saw it, but I never saw him."

"What were you doing there?"

Jesse stared him down. "Don't turn this around on me. Answer my question. Was it Keith?"

Another glance at the mirror, then: "Yes, it was Officer Clarkson."

"Oh my god." Jesse stood and pounded his fists against the wall. Tears let loose. "No. No. No. Not Keith. How did he get mixed up with Kellerman?" He looked up at the camera in the corner. "Keith. You fucked up, man. Why, why, why?"

Doherty stood behind him, set a hand on his shoulder. "I know he was a good friend of yours. I'm sorry for your loss."

"Sorry?" He turned to face the detective. "Your department hired that killer...brought him to this small town to wreak havoc—"

"So you say, but saying it and proving it are two different animals."

"The proof is in that security computer. I don't care what you have to do to break into it, send it to the FBI in Quantico, let a ten-year-old kid have a go at it...I'd even give it a shot if you'd let me..."

I'm not giving up my flash drive. It's insurance.

"Kellerman is the bad guy, not me, not Nick Fortune. How many people have to die before you get it?"

"I know you're upset, but you can't go around talking like that."

Jesse sat down, took a few deep breaths, thought of Keith... "Was his body burned up, like Fortune's?"

"Oddly, he was found in the stairwell where he bled out from a leg wound...shot through the femoral artery."

"Then Nick must've shot him...in self-defense. Kellerman went there to kill him."

"You don't know that."

"I know he was framing Nick for the attack on my sister, sent a goon squad to the Bliss to pick him up."

"I know for sure that Kellerman dragged Keith to safety, and used his belt for a tourniquet, tried to save him."

"Kellerman's no hero, I tell you. It's his fault Keith was in that gun battle in the first place. He should answer for that."

Doherty reseated himself, slapped the flat of his hand on the papers. "Kellerman's notes on the investigation...all this circumstantial evidence on a variety of suspects, but no mention of motive anywhere. Why would Kellerman have it in for you and your sister?"

Jim Keane

"You're the detective. I'm just in the middle of this bucket of shit, swimming for my life. Maybe NYPD knows something about him that your department doesn't know."

A knock at the door, Doherty stood to open it. It was the duty sergeant. "His lawyer is here."

"He didn't ask for a lawyer."

My lawyer? Garfield?

"I'll send him away."

"Wait. I do. I want to see my lawyer."

"Imagine that." Doherty smirked. "His timing is impeccable. Send him in."

The duty sergeant stepped back and in rushed Paul Garfield, hair unkempt, tie loose, suit coat unbuttoned, and briefcase in hand. "Jesse, don't say anything more."

Doherty stood his ground. "What's the problem, counselor?"

"Is my client under arrest?"

"He's here for questioning, and I must say, our conversation has been enlightening."

"Did you Mirandize him?"

"No."

"Great." He turned to Jesse. "Nothing you've said here can be used against you in a court of law."

"That's a relief."

"You haven't incriminated yourself, right?"

"No, sir." *Good old Garfield.*

"Counselor, relax. Have a seat." Doherty offered him the vacant chair.

"He doesn't have to talk to you, detective. He's free to go, right?"

"Sit and listen."

"It's okay, Paul." Jesse pointed to the chair. "I want your opinion of Doherty here. Can he be trusted?"

"Cops can't be trusted, none of them. It's their job to put you behind bars. Let's get out of here before you say something stupid."

"Come on, Paul. Sit down."

Garfield sat and frowned. "Okay, Doherty. What questions do you have for my client?"

Doherty sat in his chair. "I'm not accusing your client of anything, however, he's accusing Detective Kellerman of being a killer."

"He's in the hospital, I hear."

"Same one as my sister," Jesse put in. "And he's going to kill her if he gets half a chance."

"You see the problem here, counselor? All talk, no proof."

Garfield huffed. "Kellerman has no proof my client laid a hand on him, but he's buffaloed the DA into pressing charges. Explain that one, detective."

"A lot of finger-pointing going on here. Speculation, as well. I still need a motive."

"I guess you have your work cut out for you, detective." Garfield stood. "Come on, Jesse. We're out of here."

"Don't leave town."

"Cops always say that."

Outside, Jesse spotted Rory in his cab. "Looks like my ride his here, Paul. Thanks for looking in on me."

"Keep your nose clean, Jesse. Your arraignment is in two days."

"Can you get the case thrown out?"

Garfield ran a hand over his face. "I've been talking to the DA. Went over that asshole Matt Johnson's head. Might get the charge knocked down to a misdemeanor disturbing the peace."

"No way. I'm not pleading to anything. Make them prove their case in court. There's no proof I hit him. Put Kellerman on the stand. Call him a liar in front of the jury."

"Calm down, Jesse. You get convicted in court, that's twenty years for assaulting a cop. You plead out, you may get a year's probation."

"The system sucks."

"Better than a stint in Sing Sing." Garfield looked up at the sky. "Ah, the life of a public defender. No fame, no glory, no appreciation."

"See you in court." Jesse got into the cab.

Rory handed him the flash drive. "You keep it. Makes me knees feel weak."

"All I know is that those cops better be able to break into that security computer, or Kellerman may walk."

"Why not give 'em the drive and be done with it?"

"As long as I have this, I have some power over Kellerman."

"Got him by the balls, do ya?"

"Let's go."

"Where to, Jess?"

"Hudson Valley Hospital. Kellerman's there and he's way too close to my sister." He dialed his mom.

"Jaysus."

She answered all in a huff. "Jesse, what's going on? We can't take much more of this."

"Kellerman is in the hospital."

"What? How?"

"Inform the security staff to be extra vigilant. Rory and I are on the way."

"When is this nightmare going to end?"

"Hang in there, Mom. With you and Francis, it's two against one. Add the guards, that's four against one. You'll be okay."

He hung up and hoped the odds on this bet were in his favor, for once.

Chapter Twenty

As the anesthesia wore off and tendrils of pain invaded his back, unforeseeable events had led him to this moment. Kellerman couldn't help but wonder if some mystical force or a greater power was at play here, driving his relentless thirst for vengeance against the man who caused his daughter's life-destroying injury.

On his journey to get revenge, his actions destined him to land in the same hospital, on the same floor, as the girl he'd tried to kill, the daughter of the cop who'd fired the wayward shot, plus her brother, effectively killing Seamus Curley's family lineage and wiping his DNA from the Earth for all time.

Revenge is sweet when it's total and complete.

It was only just, as his daughter would never give him grandchildren. With that, his lineage, his family tree had ended on a broken branch. Now, he'd been given a second chance to kill Clarissa Curley. This significant turn of events had to have divine implications. Some might argue it was a coincidence.

There are no coincidences in a police investigation.

Without intervention on his part, Clarissa Curley would recover while Deirdre remained slumped in a wheelchair with drool dripping from her mouth. Now, he'd found himself in the unique position to finish what he'd started. He would sneak into her ICU bay and extinguish her life, as easily as snuffing out a languid candle flame.

And then there was Jesse Curley to deal with. He'd be sentenced to prison where rival gangs would vie for reward money to kill him. Someone would shank him in the shower, but not until after the inmates had passed their 'little bitch' around. His death in prison would be slow and painful.

Kellerman lay there and pictured God looking down on him, a mere ant in the scheme of things, making his murderous plans. *Revenge is mine, sayeth Harry Kellerman.* As long as he breathed, he would not relent. The thought of his daughter in that wheelchair fueled his homicidal determination.

I have to push past the pain, get on my feet, and get the killing done.

***

Clarissa lay in her ICU bed, determined to regain control over her body. The numbness in her legs was the least of her problems. Her hands were bandaged, her fingers so stiff and unreliable she couldn't even hold a spoon.

A nurse stood by her side, feeding her Jell-O. "You'll be back to eating on your own in no time." Her eyes crinkled in the corners as she offered encouragement.

The Jell-O was cold and a comfort to her aching throat. Not being able to speak was her most frustrating concern. Lastly, she couldn't stop thinking about the most horrifying night of her life. The boogeyman was real, and he carried a big knife. Seemed she couldn't close her eyes without reliving the terror.

The Jell-O was gone.

"Good job, Clarissa." She set the cup aside and raised her finger. "Now follow my finger, but don't move your head."

She wanted to say she wasn't drunk but couldn't get out more than a weak grunt. She followed the nurse's finger back and forth. There was no problem with her eyes.

"You're doing great. Now move your toes."

This task was a bit more difficult, as the tingling interfered with the commands from her brain. The broken glass in that alley had wreaked havoc on her extremities. With effort, she wiggled something down there, hopefully a toe.

The nurse smiled reassuringly. "You'll be walking in no time."

It's all so frustrating.

The nurse's eyebrows raised a little. "Don't stress yourself over this. You've been through a lot. Your ability to speak will come back in time. The good news is there's no damage to your vocal cords. The doc said there's probably a disconnect to your brain, no doubt due to swelling. Therapy should help."

Clarissa could only nod. *I want my vocal cords to work right now.* She felt as though she had sunk in a deep sea, and she was pushing through the water toward the surface, struggling, fighting, determined to make a full recovery.

The nurse placed a straw to Clarissa's lips. She had no trouble sucking the grape Kool-Aid into her mouth and swallowing. *But why can't I speak?*

The nurse set aside the hospital-sized sippy-cup and moved toward the gap in the curtain. "I'll check back later." She strode out.

Mom and Uncle Francis appeared above her. The worry on their faces didn't go unnoticed. "Get some rest, baby girl."

I'm not a baby, Mom. She closed her eyes and exhaled in exasperation. Visions came out of the darkness: the hulk of a man, the masked face, the blade of a knife coming at her... A shot of adrenaline forced her to open her eyes wide. Her heart was thumping like mad.

She screamed and screamed and screamed.

***

Jesse and Rory arrived at the hospital and parked in the VISITORS lot. Rory turned off the engine. "That was it? Garfield got you out of there with no problem?"

"Cops respect lawyers, but there's one thing Doherty said that stuck with me. Motivation. Why would Kellerman want to kill Clarissa? Why would he file false charges against me?"

"He's an arsehole."

"Yeah. You'll get no argument from me there. Maybe I can find something about him on the internet. For all we know, he may have been a dirty cop somewhere else, like the NYPD for starters."

Upstairs at the nurses' station to the ICU, Jesse corralled the duty nurse. "I need to use a computer that has internet access."

"This isn't the library, Mr. Curley. These computers are for official hospital business only."

"Hmmm." He looked around. "Do you know anyone who has a personal laptop?"

"Clem has an iPad," another nurse interjected. "He only uses it to watch porn."

Jesse grumped. "Can you pry it out of his hands for a few minutes?"

"He's an orderly. I'll have to run him down."

"I'll be in with my sister."

She hit the door button.

Jesse stopped at the door guards. "Rory, I'll see you inside," then he addressed the guards. "Did you get the word that Kellerman is here...in this hospital?"

"Don't worry. He won't get past us."

"I thank you, and my sister thanks you." He hurried into the ICU and through the gap in curtain number two. "Mom, Francis. How's she doing?"

"Sleeping. They have her heavily sedated."

Francis added, "She had some kind of mental breakdown."

Rory stood at the foot of the bed. "She is lookin' better."

"She still can't speak," Jude said. "A speech therapist is supposed to see her, after she's transferred to a private room, hopefully this afternoon."

"Getting out of ICU. That's an improvement."

A nurse stepped in with a laptop. "Jesse, you wanted this?"

"Oh, yes. Thanks."

"Clem says to be careful with it. There's stuff in here that can break the internet."

"I'll bet."

Francis stepped up. "What are you going to do with that?"

"Kellerman has to have a back story. He didn't come to this small town from out of a vacuum. Maybe I can find a motive for him targeting us...our family."

"Let's have a look."

Jesse set the laptop on the over-bed table and swung it into position in front of them. He clicked on the browser. Multiple windows opened: *VIRUS ALERT,* and *THREATS FOUND,* and the largest with a flashing red border: *WARNING. Your computer has been corrupted. Call 1800WEGOTYOU for technical assistance.* Jesse felt as though he should wash his hands.

Rory joined him and Francis. "A wee bit of mischief, huh?"

Jesse clicked off the windows then used Google to search for Harry Kellerman. A bunch of nonsense came up: *a ballet instructor in Arizona, Harry Trotter in the Fifth at Churchill Downs, Dirty Harry...* He tried again, this time by typing *Harold Kellerman NYPD.* The official NYPD website listed him as a homicide detective RETIRED. The accompanying brief bio was no help... *Wait.* ...lives on Long Island with his wife Kathleen and daughter Deirdre.

I wonder where they are now?

He typed *Kathleen Kellerman,* came up with an obituary that talked of her *untimely death after a severe bout of depression.*

Francis huffed.

"Depressed?" Rory said over Jesse's shoulder. "What about? Does it say?"

"Says: *She is survived by her husband, Harold, and daughter Deirdre, paralyzed during a gang shootout with police.*"

"Getting close to home," Francis said.

That possibility spurred Jesse's heart rate into overtime. He typed in his father's name: *Seamus Curley NYPD...* Again, the official site came up, and his bio ended with *died in the line of duty.*

At that brush with the truth, Jesse took offense. "Died? He was ambushed...murdered..."

"It's a cold case now," Francis added.

Jesse typed in *Deirdre Kellerman* to find out what happened to her. Nothing of any value came up. He typed *gang warfare in New York City* and found page after page of incidents and newspaper articles.

Francis sighed. "It's a killing field."

Strolling through the articles, he stopped at one from the New York Post, a tabloid of sorts: GIRL CRITICAL AFTER GANG SHOOTOUT WITH POLICE. "Could it be her?" Reading further: *spinal injury, may never walk again,* no name was given, only stating she was the *daughter of an NYPD Lieutenant.*

"Mom..." Jesse turned around, saw her slumped in the accent chair beside Francis, clearly exhausted. "Did NYPD ever release the name of the girl who was wounded in that shootout, the one Dad got in all that trouble over?"

"The family wanted to remain anonymous for privacy reasons. Can't say I blame them. Tragic. Your dad was never the same."

"I think it was Kellerman's daughter, and he may not have agreed with the 'accidental' part of the report, turned vigilante, I bet. He's probably the guy who ambushed Dad in his squad car."

Doherty's words came back to him: *Saying it and proving it are two different animals.*

Francis said, "Revenge is a dish best served cold."

Jude reached up and smacked his arm. "What does that even mean?"

Jesse questioned something else. "But why us? Clarissa and I had nothing to do with it."

"A mental break. He's gone plum crazy."

"Crazy like a fox." Jesse shut down the browser. A window came up, lit and flashing like a theater marquee:

GIRLS! GIRLS! GIRLS! No credit card needed.

Rory harrumphed. "Clem must be a real fun lad."

Jesse closed the lid. "Rory. Do me a large. Go back to the station and tell Doherty we have Kellerman's motive. Revenge. Tell him to look into it, and ask him to find the daughter. I'll bet she's in a facility nearby. I'm staying here to give my mom and Francis a break. They need to sleep for a while."

"I'm on it, laddy." He turned to leave but Jesse stopped him.

"Wait." He held out the laptop. "Give this garbage to the duty nurse. Tell her to tell Clem we said thanks."

"Do I have to touch it?"

"Here..." Jesse tucked it under Rory's sleeved arm, and he was off.

"So, Jesse." Jude sat up straight. "You think all this mayhem has to do with your dad's part in that gang shootout?"

"That'll be for Detective Doherty to decide. I'm only guessing."

"Your father would roll over in his grave if he knew that terrible accident resulted in harm to his children."

"I'm sure you're right, Mom. Go home and get some rest."

"I'd rather stay here."

"Come on, sis. Up and at em." Francis helped her to her feet and escorted her out.

Jesse took her place in the cushy chair. Yeah. He was beat, too, but sleep was a luxury he could not afford, not with Kellerman under the same roof as Clarissa.

***

Kellerman groaned. He'd managed to drag himself out of bed and stagger-step to the wheelchair. He'd convinced the nurse to leave it in his room in case he had to do #2, a job much better done in the toilet across the room rather than in a bedpan. His back felt like it was coated in cement and anchored in place with steel spikes.

Goddamned Fortune and his fragmentation grenade.

He wheeled himself into the corridor and turned right. From previous forays down the hall for the purpose of exercise, he'd learned the location of the ICU and the door the medical staff used. Having monitored the nurses' comings and goings, he knew their routines. He had ten minutes to get to Clarissa and exact his revenge...*for my Deirdre, my only daughter.*

He edged toward the ICU, every push on the wheels' handrims a battle against the pain that coursed through his body. A nurse passed by and he nodded. An orderly was more troublesome. "Let me push the chair for you. Where are we going?" *To the ICU to murder a patient.* He declined the offer. "I need the exercise."

At the staff entrance to the ICU, which had no markings that said as much, he ran into his first roadblock, an array of yellow WET FLOOR cones. An overweight janitor wearing a grey outfit was slopping water on the floor. "You can't come through here, buddy."

"I just want to visit someone in there."

"Not unless it's an emergency. Hospital rules, ya know. Safety first. You gotta wait 'til this floor dries."

Shit. By that time, they'd discover him missing from his room. He gripped the armrests of the wheelchair and ground his teeth. *I need to get by this guy...* If he charged on through, he'd draw unwanted attention.

Fuck.

He turned the wheelchair around and retreated

to his room. As expected, he'd no sooner crawled back into bed when the nurse wheeled in a laptop tray to take his vitals.

She consulted the computer screen. "How are you feeling, Lieutenant?"

He had to fight to calm his breathing. "Getting better."

She put a gun to his head and pulled the trigger. "Ah... your temperature is normal." She set the temp gun on the tray and unrolled an arm cuff. Velcro-strapped in place, she used a hand pump to pump, pump, pump it up. Tight, very tight, but he was too tough to complain. Her eyebrows rose as she watched the gauges. "Your blood pressure is high. One eighty over ninety. That's not good, sugar."

"I feel fine."

"You look a little winded. I should call the doctor."

Hot anger surged through his body. How easy it would be to grab her by the neck and choke the livin' shit out of her. "I said I'm fine."

"Calm down, sir. You're going to suffer a stroke."

She typed into the laptop. "Doc should be here in twenty minutes."

"You didn't have to go and do that."

"You're not dying on my watch, no sir. We don't take any chances around here." She wheeled her stuff out.

Alright. He sat up and surveyed the corridor. The way was clear. Shifting from the bed to the wheelchair was torture. He rolled out of the room again, relentless, and unstoppable.

Two nurses chatted at an intersection down the hall. They paid him no mind as he wheeled past them. At the ICU door, the janitor was gone, but he'd left a CAUTION WET FLOOR cone standing guard...for safety.

He pushed through the swinging doors and rolled forward with no time to lose. His arms ached from exertion. He reached curtain number two, wheeled through the gap, and stopped beside the bed. A pile of blankets concealed her, but not for long. Standing, he cracked his knuckles and couldn't wait to see the look on her face... He threw off the blankets.

What the fuck?

She was gone.

An orderly stepped in. "What are you doing in here?"

Whirling with a groan, he faced the guy, his Paul Bunyan arms crossed like Superman. "I...ah...

He was suddenly ten years old again, his mother

standing over him in that same pose. A cigarette dangled from her mouth. "What are you doing in here, young man?"

Dumbfounded with his mouth open, he didn't know what to say. The cookie jar fell off the table. Shattered. He was busted, red-handed.

She slapped him across the face. "I'm talking to you, boy. You know you're not supposed to be in the kitchen, sneaking around and stealing cookies."

He wiggled his tongue, tasted blood.

"Do I have to call security?"

"Ah...no. I came to visit the patient who was here."

"And I'm here to clean up for the next one."

"But where's Clarissa?"

"She's been moved to a private room. Now, get out of here so I can do my job." He pulled back the curtain, revealing the entire ICU.

Kellerman gave the wheelchair a spin and raced to the back door, arms burning.

Now what am I going to do? This whole revenge thing is turning into a bucket of shit with the handles on the inside.

Chapter Twenty-One

ack at the precinct, phones rang. Cops hustled about. Radios crackled. The station had transformed into a maelstrom of chaos. Officer Clarkson's death had rattled the entire department, and Internal Affairs' shoot team was in an uproar. The arson squad was combing the debris at Hudson Valley Condos, and the ATF had questions about the M67 grenade that caused the explosion. Reports were stacking up on Doherty's desk.

"Welcome back from vacation," the Duty Sergeant said. "Got a cabbie out here wants to talk to you about the Curley assault."

"Kellerman has already interviewed him. What's he want?"

"He has a message from Jesse Curley."

"Not him again."

"You want to talk to the cabbie or not?"

"Damnit anyway." Doherty slammed his hand on the desk, scattering papers. "Send him in."

Doherty had inherited two cases: Clarissa Curley's attack and the killings at Fortune's apartment. Retirement was a pipedream; he had two young daughters, and the need to fund their college education kept him chained to this job.

A knock, and the cabbie stepped in through the open doorway. "Sorry to be a bother, sir." He held a green cap. "Jesse asked me to deliver a message."

"Then out with it, man. I'm busy."

"Ya wanted a motive for Kellerman's assault on Clarissa Curley...it's revenge, sir. In New York City, his daughter was paralyzed by a stray bullet shot from a NYPD cop's gun during a gangland shootout. That would be Officer Seamus Curley, Jesse and Clarissa's father." He gave the cap a little flip. "Kellerman's daughter should be in a facility nearby. Jesse thought you should find her to verify what he found online."

Doherty was flabbergasted. "Man, you need to go back to driving a cab and leave the investigating to professionals. None of what you said makes any sense."

"I'm telling ya what we learned. It's up to you bobbies to make sense of it."

"Get out of here. You're wasting my time."

"Yes, sir..."

The phone interrupted him, and he gruffly answered, "Detective Doherty."

Jim Keane

"Hey, detective, this is Grimes from Forensics."

"Tell me some good news for a change." He leaned back in his chair. "You broke into the Bliss security computer?"

"No, sir. The Duty Sergeant said you were asking about it, thought I'd give you an update."

"Update? Call me when you're in. I've got to see those videos?" He slammed down the phone and looked up Rory. "Why are you still here?"

"Just wondering... do ya want me to ask Jesse to give it a shot? He's an IT tech from Vericom, ya know."

"Our lab boys are the best. They'll get into it."

Rory shrugged and turned away.

"Tell Jesse thanks. Okay?"

"Gladly." He set on his cap and was gone.

Without seeing the so-called video proof of Kellerman's involvement in the assault, Doherty had nothing to go on. However, if Kellerman was guilty, maybe...

He stood and rushed to the Captain's office. A knock. "Sir, a word?"

"Detective. How was vacation?"

"Short. I need to ask Kellerman about the Curley case, at the hospital. Get a look into his eyes. Gage his reaction."

"Are you onto something?"

"I don't know, but from what outside sources are telling me, it might rattle this department to its core."

"Then walk lightly, detective. Make no mistakes."

"Yes, sir."

Back in his office, Doherty pulled on his suit coat over his shoulder-holstered service revolver, and slipped the lanyard badge around his neck. *It's showtime.*

***

Doherty used the main entrance into Hudson Valley Hospital and stepped up to a busy information desk. He flashed his badge and drew immediate attention from a security staffer. "Can I help you, sir?"

"Detective Harold Kellerman's room number, please."

The man checked a monitor. "That would be 314 in the emergency ward."

"How is he?"

"Says here, hmmm, post-surgery observation pending possible admission."

"So he might be released?"

"Not for me to speculate. Ask the duty nurse. Elevators to your left, third floor to your right."

"Got it, thanks."

As he boarded the elevator to Kellerman's floor, his thoughts centered on the detective's purported motive. It went against the belief and creed that the police were all part of the same team despite different departments and precincts in separate cities.

One blue wall.

Had Detective Kellerman forgotten this basic premise?

What secrets was he keeping?

The elevator opened to the sound of shouting down the hallway to the right. Nearing Kellerman's room, the loud voices intensified. He quickened his pace and found a wheelchair-bound Kellerman and a nurse in front of 314, engaged in a heated confrontation.

"What do you think you're doing out here?"

"I was just getting some exercise."

"Where did you go?"

"Down the hall a bit and back again."

"I told you to stay in bed, and you're not to be wandering around without a nurse or orderly present. You could have a stroke..."

They turned to look at Doherty, mouths suddenly clamped shut.

"What's the problem?"

The nurse huffed. "He doesn't listen to the doctors' orders."

"I'm not an invalid."

"You're impossible."

Doherty held out a hand. *Stop.* "I'll take it from here, ma'am."

She stormed off while he pushed the wheelchair into the room. "I need to ask you about something."

"Help me get back in bed."

"You're fine right where you are." He parked the wheelchair and set the brake. "Tell me about your daughter."

His face turned ashen with shock.

"Is she paralyzed?"

His eyes widened as if his mind got tangled in a maze, and his breathing deepened. Doherty noticed a tremor in Kellerman's hand, which he'd countered with a fist.

"Did I hit a nerve there, detective?"

His brows hooded his eyes in anger. "How dare you ask me about her? She's none of your damn business."

"So it's true."

"Get out of my room."

"Where is she, Harold?"

"Fuck you." Kellerman pushed up out of the

wheelchair and dragged himself onto the bed, where he began frantically pressing the nurses' call button.

"Does the name Seamus Curley ring any bells?"

"I'm warning you." His face was mottled with rage.

"So that's a yes. Where is your daughter?"

"Leave her alone, or I'll kill your goddamned ass."

That same nurse ran in. "What's the matter now?"

"Seems I just rattled his cage."

"Get out. Get him out of here." Kellerman was thrashing around like a crazy man.

The nurse tried to hold him down. "Please, detective, help me."

Doherty joined the fray, pressed down on Kellerman's left shoulder while the nurse struggled with his arms.

It happened so fast...

#

Kellerman's rage would not be tamped, but as always, he didn't let anything slip his attention. Not the lanyard badge hanging over him, not the wide-open suit coat, not the holstered gun.

He shoved the nurse back, grabbed the lanyard and yanked Doherty's face to his while his free hand grabbed the gun. Doherty pushed against his shoulder, trying to get away, but the lanyard held and the gun came out. Safety off, he growled in Doherty's ear. "You should have stayed on vacation." He pulled the trigger. *Bang.* And let go of the lanyard.

Doherty staggered back, eyes wide. A red bloom grew on his shirt. The nurse screamed as he fell to the floor.

Having come this far, Kellerman saw no reason to stop. Now, he could complete his revenge for Deirdre, though he might never see her again. He swiveled the gun to the nurse, "Don't move," and levered himself off the bed.

"You shot him. You killed him. Are you fucking crazy?"

He seized her by her white collar and put the gun to her head. "Clarissa Curley's room. Stat."

"No. No, please—"

"Shut up, and you just might live through this."

***

In Clarissa's private room, Jesse jumped at the sound of a gunshot from somewhere down the hall. The sound was so clear, and so foreign to a hospital environment, he knew trouble was on the way. A quick glance at his sister, wide-eyed and staring, told him she'd heard it too. His mom and Francis were still at home, sleeping and safe.

An announcement blared over the PA: *"Security to Zone Three. Code red."*

He sprinted to the door and looked down the hallway.

Nothing.

No wait. A nurse appeared from around a corner, followed by Kellerman, tight behind her, holding a gun barrel to her head. She looked ghostly white with fear. His red-faced rage told Jesse to run.

He ducked back inside, rushed to the bed. "Clarissa, we gotta go. He dragged her out of bed, but her bandaged feet wouldn't support her. It took all his strength to hold up her dead weight. He finally had to set her on the floor. "Can you crawl?"

Then: "Where do you think you're going?"

Kellerman was right behind him. He turned keeping low and his body in front of Clarissa. "Leave her alone."

He shoved the petrified nurse to the floor. "What do you know? Both Curley's in one fell swoop."

The nurse whimpered. "Don't hurt them."

Kellerman kicked the door shut. "Finally. Sweet, sweet revenge." He raised the gun.

"I know about your daughter," Jesse shouted, his hands up. "I know what happened."

"You know nothing."

"She's paralyzed. A vegetable. And a bullet from my dad's gun was responsible. We're so sorry, but how many lives will you destroy before you call it even?"

"Two more and the slate is clean."

"No," the nurse screamed and swung a leg around to kick Kellerman in the shin.

That had to hurt.

He staggered back, "Bitch," and swung the gun to her.

Jesse didn't take the time to think, just lunged at him, full-force into his arm and throwing both of them into the wall. The gun clattered to the floor. Jesse got in two kidney punches.

Kellerman hollered, tossed him to the floor, and dove for the gun.

Jesse kicked it, and it spun and skidded toward the bed.

Kellerman came down on Jesse like a WWE wrestler from the top rope. The impact knocked the breath out of his lungs, and his vision blinked on and off like a faulty bulb in a dark cellar. A fist walloped him a good one. The coppery taste of blood filled his mouth.

Kellerman stood and kicked him in the ribs.

"This is for Deirdre," and he kicked him again.

Bang!

Breathless and bloody, Jesse looked up, saw the man teeter, stagger, and fall. In his wacked out vision, it seemed like a blur, and he glanced at the door, expecting a cop, but the door was still closed. He shifted his gaze to Clarissa on the floor, shakily pointing the gun at Kellerman as smoke wisped from the barrel.

"Clarissa." He dragged himself to her and took the gun from her bandaged hands.

The nurse was up and out the door, screaming down the corridor.

"I...shot...him," Clarissa said. "I shot him."

"You shot him." Jesse gasped. "Oh, my god, you can speak."

"I can."

He hugged her. "You're going to be alright."

They both started happily bawling.

Nurses, doctors, orderlies, and cops rushed in. A doctor checked Kellerman. "I've got a pulse. ER stat."

An orderly rolled in a gurney. It took four people to lift him up, and then they rushed him away.

Two nurses and Jesse got Clarissa back into bed. "Where's Mom and Uncle Francis?" she asked.

It was so good to hear her voice again. "I'll call

Mom right away. You just relax."

"I almost died in that alley, Jess. Then Kellerman came at me with a pillow. I thought I was a goner."

"I know, but he's done for now."

"Thanks for looking out for me."

"Don't mention it."

"Do you think the doctors can save him?"

"Frankly, sis. I don't give a shit."

Chapter Twenty-Two

Jesse and Clarissa attended the funeral for Officer Keith Clarkson. Squad cars and motorcycles were lined up for miles. Policemen came from all around: Peekskill, NYPD, New York State Police, Westchester, and more. Each wore badges with a strip of black tape across them. A flag-draped coffin sat on a bier before a wreathed photo of a smiling Keith in his dress blues.

The sorrow and heartbreak was palpable.

Garbed in full robes, Father O'Leary, beefy with broad shoulders and red cheeks, strode to the podium. "We are gathered here today to pay our respects to one of our bravest public servants."

The crowd sniffled and sobbed. "Amen, Father."

"Dear Lord. We know it's too early to lose Keith Clarkson, but we trust in you, your judgment and your will, which will be done on Earth as it is in Heaven."

Keith's parents hugged each other, sobbing.

"Keith never shirked his responsibility. He met the challenge of law enforcement head-on with eyes wide open. He's a credit to himself and all police officers who serve and protect. The bond within the police community is strong, whether they know each other or not. Each of them face danger daily. They all have one thing in common. Any day on the job could be their last, as it was with Keith Clarkson, who gave his life in the line of duty."

The police officers nodded with hands on each other's shoulders.

"They have gathered here as one police force today, one brotherhood to say goodbye to their fallen brother. God, we ask that you bless Keith's soul, that he may stand by your side in paradise."

Jesse truly believed that Keith deserved that much, and a tear in his eye bore witness to his conviction. And for that matter, there wasn't a dry eye in the sanctuary...well...except for Conrad, who stood in the back, glaring at him.

I'll never get that monkey off my back.

***

Nick Fortune's service was held later that evening, more of a wake, a party to celebrate his life, of which the Bliss had played a huge part. His brother had flown in from Miami to open the nightclub, and he'd asked the bartender and the barmaids, Ginger and Sylvia, to stay on and keep the place hopping.

Jesse was honored to accept the position of manager. Nick Fortune's legacy would live on in Peekskill.

A special guest attended the party, Detective Sam Doherty, patched up and on his feet after being gut-shot by Kellerman, who was now confined to the high-security ward and guarded 24/7 until he was fit enough to be transferred to county jail to await trial. His legacy as the small-town killer would rot in prison with him.

***

With all that had transpired in Peekskill, Jesse's arraignment on the charge of assaulting a police officer finally got underway. He sat in the defendant's chair, at a table next to the prosecutor's table. The defense lawyer's chair was vacant, as was the DA's chair. The courtroom buzzed with activity as town residents filed in. Jude and Francis sat in the gallery behind him, along with Clarissa, on the mend, and Rory, green cap and all.

Having a vested interest in the outcome, Conrad loomed in the back row, eyes narrowed, arms folded, crushing a fat wad of tobacco between his teeth.

A cold sweat broke out on Jesse's brow despite the room's warmth. The air hung with anticipation amplified by the occasional whisper or cough.

The bailiff stood at the front, and a court reporter

sat at the clerk's table, ready to type.

Where's Garfield? He turned to the back of the courtroom, searching for his lawyer, but he was MIA.

Conrad scowled at him.

Jesse's throat tightened. What else could go wrong?

The courthouse doors swung open, and in walked DA Matt Johnson, dressed in a suit. He strode by him to his chair, set down a briefcase, and ignored Jesse.

Prick.

The doors behind the judge's raised table opened, and the judge came in.

"All rise," the bailiff commanded. "The court is now in session, the honorable Judge Delaney presiding."

Johnson glowered at Jesse. "Where's your lawyer?"

The judge sat. "Quiet, everyone. Mr. Curley, where is your attorney?"

Jesse shuddered under the judge's harsh glare. "I don't know, your Honor."

The judge's face flushed. "Does the state wish to proceed with this arraignment?"

Johnson stood. "Yes, your honor."

Jesse swallowed hard.

The judge struck his gavel. "Very well. Mr. Curley, do you understand the charge against you?"

A commotion stirred in the gallery.

Jesse looked back to see Garfield fast-stepping in through the door, stuffing papers into his briefcase, a balancing act worthy of the price of admission. Out of breath, he sat next to Jesse. "Sorry I'm late, your Honor."

With a glare and folded arms, the judge checked his watch. "Glad you could make it, counselor."

Garfield fixed his hair and straightened his tie. "I got delayed by another client."

"I'm sure you did, Mr. Garfield, but don't do it again." The judge shook his head. "I've just finished asking your client if he understood the charge against him?"

Garfield stood. "He does, yes, of course."

"Assault on a police officer."

"Yes."

"Does your client understand that is a felony with a lengthy prison sentence, upwards of twenty years, plus a hefty fine?"

"Yes." Garfield nodded to the DA, then: "Your Honor, we move to dismiss."

Jesse pursed his lips. *Give them hell, Garfield.*

"Dismiss?" The judge's eyebrows shot up. "On

what grounds?"

"Detective Kellerman isn't a credible plaintiff. He's under arrest for three counts of attempted murder, two on Clarissa Curley, one on our own Detective Doherty, assault on the defendant, and kidnapping a nurse by force, for starters."

The judge turned to District Attorney Johnson. "What does the state have to say?"

Johnson straightened some papers and stood. "Mr. Garfield is correct. We have Detective Kellerman in custody."

The judge frowned. "I see. It's unfortunate when one of our trusted protectors is himself a criminal." He turned to the defense. "Do you have anything to add?"

"There's no evidence to substantiate the charge against my client, only Kellerman's testimony, which is unreliable, if not fabricated."

"As for the motion to dismiss, Mr. Johnson, what does the state have to say in this matter?"

"We're willing to drop the charges, your Honor, for lack of evidence."

Yes. Relief cascaded over Jesse. *Good job, Garfield.*

The judge banged his gavel and stood. "The defendant is free to go."

The bailiff shouted, "All rise."

As the judge retired, chatter erupted from the gallery.

DA Matt Johnson closed his briefcase and stood to offer Garfield a handshake. "I'll get you next time."

Garfield grinned. "Wouldn't miss it for the world."

"Oh, by the way. Detective Morrison came to us with some bullshit attempted bank robbery charge on your client. We declined to prosecute for lack of evidence. He actually seemed grateful."

"Kellerman probably put him up to it."

"Yeah. We're going to put that dirty cop away for a long time."

"You won't see me defending him."

"Catch you at the club." Johnson walked out with a little skip in his step.

Jesse stood, somewhat stupefied. Seemed like Garfield and Johnson, fierce competitors in the courtroom, were actually good friends.

Outside in the hallway, Jesse's mom, Uncle Francis, Clarissa, and Rory were waiting for him. Congratulatory back slaps went all around. He noticed Clarissa's bunny slippers. "Hey, you're on your feet."

"I'm here for you. What's a little pain matter?"

Then the spoiler barged in. Conrad grabbed him

by the collar and whipped him around. "Where's my money, loser?"

Uncle Francis stepped up. "Let go of my nephew before I snap you in half like a dry breadstick."

"He owes me, man. Just trying to collect on a bad bet."

"What don't you understand? Did I stutter? Let him go."

Rory bulled his way in, rolling up his sleeves. "I got your back, Jesse." He put up his dukes. "Let's dance, broc."

Conrad let go but not without giving Jesse a shove. "Sooner or later, loser..." he cracked his knuckles, "your ass is grassed."

Francis raised his eyebrows. "Jesse, why are you doing business with this thug?"

"Bookies are hard to come by in a small town."

His mom scowled. "Jesse. I'm disappointed in you. When are you going to learn? Gambling—"

"Gambling is a sin, I know, Mom." Jesse winced under her stern critique.

"It's the devil's business. See? You're looking at one of his demons, this Conrad fella."

Conrad smirked as if he didn't take offense.

"How much do you owe this guy?" Francis asked.

Jesse sighed. "Ten thousand."

Uncle Francis's eyes enlarged. "When you fuck up, you go all the way." He addressed Conrad. "Will you settle for five?"

Conrad's forehead rippled. "He bet on the Yankees like a damn fool. They never win when you need them to, isn't that right, Jesse? You've got to pay for that stupidity."

"I was unemployed, broke and desperate. You told me it was a sure bet."

"Aaron The Judge had been on his game all season. How was I to know he'd choke in the 9th?"

Francis frowned. "So, it's your fault he made the bet?"

"A bet's a bet. Your boy is delinquent. I've got expenses, you know."

"Alright, here's the deal. I'll pay you five, call it square, unless my boy Jesse here, places another bet. Then he's fair game for owing you the other five Gs."

Jesse scowled. "Oh, isn't that just great. The next bet I place, I automatically lose five grand?"

Conrad smiled. "I can live with that."

"Well, Jess. It looks like your gamblin' days are done." Francis laughed.

"I'll pay you back, I swear."

"I don't want your money, Jess. I want you to

stop gambling."

"That should do it, I guess. Besides, I'm working now, and who knows, Vericom might hire me back someday. I'm a much better IT guy than a gambler, anyway."

Clarissa hooked her arm in his. "And not a bad detective, either."

Jim Keane

Epilogue

In the days, weeks, and months after the arraignment, life went on in Peekskill, a small town with big-city wounds. Doherty made Captain, penned a hero for exposing the dirty cop, Harry Kellerman, and the Bliss Nightclub was more popular than ever. Every town needed a hero and a villain and a safe place to party. Jesse managed the bar for Nick's brother, Rick Fortune, and finally learned the bartender's name, Cliff Jenkins. They were a family, or sorts, with Ginger and Sylvia their ever-popular barmaids, and Jesse at the helm.

One particularly warm winter's day, he picked up Clarissa from her psychiatric appointment for lunch, and he drove her to the Peekskill Hometown Diner. He was driving the club's Mercedes E350, Nick's ride, to which he now was privy. The old Corolla finally retired to the bone yard.

"How was therapy today?" Jesse ventured.

"Painful." She gazed out the window at the homes and businesses on Crompond Road.

He turned south on Washington. "Are you

having fewer nightmares?"

"It's always the same thing...he gets out of prison. I run. He catches me, and it's that night in the alley all over again."

"It's just a bad dream. Don't let it dictate the rest of your life."

"Easily said by one who wasn't nearly stabbed to death."

He turned into the diner drive and parked. "It's about time to get over it, don't you think."

"I do miss the club...and Tommy, too, but I can't take the chance he'll get out and attack me again."

"So you lock yourself inside your apartment? That's no way to live."

"That's for me to say and you to butt out."

"I'm betting you'll get over that fear someday...when the right motivation comes along."

"Don't hold your breath."

Inside, Mr. Pappas seated them in a booth. "We're serving brunch until two o'clock. Enjoy your meal, kids."

Thelma approached, coffee carafe in hand. "I haven't seen you two together for quite some time. What'll you have?"

"Toast and tea," Clarissa said. "Wheat and Oolong."

"That's all?" Jesse reached out to touch Clarissa's hand. "You can get whatever you want. I've got you covered."

She pulled her hand away. "I want toast and tea, Mr. Big-Shot I've-got-a-job-now-and-can-pay."

He laughed. "How the tables have turned."

Thelma asked Jesse, "And what for you, honey?"

"Your bacon, egg, and cheese omelet with hot sauce and some of that coffee."

"Ah, big spender." She poured coffee. "I'll be back with that tea."

Clarissa's panicked eyes darted about the patrons, as if Kellerman might leap from the crowd, wielding a knife.

"Sis, relax. Kellerman will never see daylight again."

"What makes you so sure?"

"Where's that optimistic girl who was ready to take on the world? Come to the club. Let loose a little."

Thelma returned with the tea.

"A night out will do you good."

Clarissa pulled the tea cup towards her and stared into the depths of the dark water as if she might drown.

"You need to hang out with your friends, get

back in the groove."

"I'm never going back to that club."

"It's a place to start."

"Did you take me to lunch to badger me?"

Toast and omelet delivered, Jesse decided to tell her why he'd asked her here. "Actually, I want you to go with me somewhere."

"Like...where?"

"Hudson Valley Children's Sanctum. That's where Detective Doherty found Kellerman's daughter, Deirdre."

"You have to be kidding."

"It might help us to understand Kellerman...why he hates us so much to want us dead."

Her eyes narrowed. "The family kept her name a secret for a reason, Jess. Anonymity. It wasn't Dad's fault what happened. We should leave it be."

"I know, but humor me. Doherty has already set it up."

"Deirdre, huh? Such a pretty name."

"Is tomorrow alright with you?"

***

And so it was that on a snowy day, Jesse and Clarissa drove to the Hudson Valley Children's Sanctum, took the tree-lined drive that led to the facility where Kellerman had secreted his daughter away. Inside, it wasn't some dark and scary place, but painted in bright colors, the walls awash in yellows and greens with flowers and cartoon animals flourishing among sunbeams and rainbows. The scent of flowers drifted in the air.

At the reception desk, Jesse spoke to a woman whose cheery smile seemed well practiced. "I called yesterday. We're here to see Deirdre Kellerman...er...Dodson."

"Yes, of course. Detective Doherty filled us in on what happened." She led the way down a bright corridor where painted ladybugs and caterpillars lined the buffed floor. At an open door, she stopped. "Deirdre, honey. You have company." The woman whispered to Jesse, "Such a shame about her father. Go ahead on in." She stepped aside.

Jesse took Clarissa's hand and braved the threshold of a life denied. A tall-backed wheelchair stacked with medical equipment was parked in front of a lone window, the drapes parted, facing outward to a snow-covered lawn and stands of barren trees. The *pop* and *wheeze* of a ventilator was the only sound. A quick scan of the room revealed a small bed with butterflies on the blanket, stuffed animals looking on, and a basketball on a shelf next to a studio photo of Kellerman and a pretty lady with raven hair and deep brown eyes. *Must be her mom.* Crystal vases on the headboard and dresser sported splays of flowers that filled the room with fragrance and color.

Pop. Wheeze. Pop. Wheeze.

Jesse made momentary eye contact with Clarissa, then: "Deirdre...hello?" He expected the wheelchair to spin around and reveal its occupant, but it didn't move.

"Maybe she's asleep," Clarissa whispered.

"She's paralyzed, but I assume she can hear. Why else would the nurse talk to her?"

Clarissa nonchalantly strode to the window and looked out. "It's pretty, Deirdre, don't you think? A winter wonderland."

There was no response from her.

"Maybe she's just shy." Jesse stepped up to join Clarissa taking in the view. "We should build a snowman."

No response.

He turned to see a frail and gaunt little girl, her head tilted nearly to her shoulder, eyes wide, greasy, and distant. A white corrugated tube was taped to her throat, and saliva dripped in gooey strands to a bib she wore. At first, his brain couldn't grasp what his eyes were seeing, but a breath later, he realized she was worse off than just paralyzed.

Jim Keane

Behind him, Clarissa gasped. "Oh, my God."

The girl's fingers were curled into her palms, which she held close to her chest. She wore a pink and white blouse, red jogging pants with white stripes, and white tennis shoes...as if she were about to go out for a run around the park. *And pigtails.* With yellow ribbons, the caregivers had tied her hair in the cutest pigtails...but truth be told, no amount of fashion and coiffing could disguise the horrific condition of the little girl within.

There seemed no limit to the depth of the pit in Jesse's stomach. "It was an accident."

"Heartbreaking...and maddening enough to drive any father to seek revenge." Clarissa turned away, her gaze back to the white scene outside the window and her eyes tearing up. "Accident or not..." she sobbed, "it doesn't change the fact that her life is ruined."

Jesse turned and looped an arm around her waist. "Now I understand Kellerman." His eyes burned with new tears. He hugged her, and they both wept together.

Pop. Wheeze. Pop. Wheeze.

***

That night, safe within the walls of her apartment, Clarissa couldn't get the image of that poor little girl out of her head. In the shower, she cried. *Why? Why? Why am I filled with all this sadness*...the feeling of being lost without a compass, afraid of every shadow? Now, naked and staring into the bathroom mirror, she took a good look at herself, her reality, her sadness invisible on the outside. She saw only the vague resemblance of a scar on her forehead, a more pronounced one on her left breast, a wound that had collapsed her lung, and an elongated scar with staple dots on her stomach where the surgeons went in to sew up her sliced intestines.

Compared to Deirdre's problems, this is nothing.

The little girl's life was wasting away, a vegetable, and the comparison to her own situation became suddenly clear.

I'm not going to waste my life. I'm going to live it to the fullest, for me, for Deirdre, and I'm going to do something good with the second chance I've been given.

Out came the makeup case, the hair dryer, and a curling wand.

I hope Tommy is there tonight.

***

A raucous crowd rolled into the Bliss. It was Friday night, and the air was electric with music and excitement. A brawny bouncer scrutinized IDs at the entrance. Surveillance cameras positioned inside and outside the club recorded all the action.

Jesse double-checked the bar's inventory. Beside him, Cliff Jenkins poured drinks for patrons sitting around the bar as well as for Ginger and Sylvia waiting at the barmaid station. The flurry of activity would've made Nick Fortune proud.

"Looks like we're in for a wild night."

By 10 p.m., the dance floor pulsated with patrons and strobe lights, and drinks flowed like a rushing river. Jesse was at the headwaters, helping Cliff handle the bar work. He'd bent to get a Corona from deep in the cooler when he heard a familiar voice call out.

"Hey, barkeep. How about a little service over here."

He looked up and saw two women had conned a couple regulars out of their stools. One was a raven-haired beauty and the other was...Clarissa.

Jesse's heart melted. *The hermit is among us.* "Clarissa. You made it."

"I'm not wasting another second of my life."

He set the Corona on Ginger's tray and joined the girls, who seemed to be pretty cozy with each other. "What are you drinking tonight?"

The girl with black hair leaned into Clarissa. "You told me you didn't have a man. The way he's smiling, I'd say you've been holding out on me."

"This is my brother Jesse. Jess, this is Eileen."

He leaned toward her with his elbows on the bar. "Why haven't I seen you in here before?"

"Your lucky night." She'd said it with a sly grin. "How about a couple margaritas? On the rocks with salt."

"Can do. Hey, Cliff, two margs over here."

Jump Around by the House of Pain blared from the DJ's speakers. "Jump Around! Jump Around! Jump up and get down!"

Jump! Jump! Jump!

The crowd roared.

"Let's go dance." Clarissa tugged Eileen off the barstool and dragged her onto the floor where they vanished amid the patrons jumping up and down.

Jesse laughed. *You go, girls.*

Rory slid into one of the vacated seats. "Ah, I've got a fierce thirst, laddy."

Jesse shook the cabby's hand. "How you been, my friend?"

"I'll be much better with a Guinness in me belly."

"On the house." Cliff slid a foamy mug down the bar, right into the Irishman's meaty mitts.

"I love this joint." Rory flipped him a five for a tip, slid off the stool, grabbed the mug's handle, and scooted off into the crowd, his green tweed cap all that was visible of him moving away.

Jump! Jump! Jump!

"Hey, Jesse." Tommy had wedged his brawn between two barstools. "I was wondering how your sister's been. Haven't seen her since she got out of the hospital."

"Clarissa? She's a trooper, back on her feet again. In fact, she's on the dance floor right now."

"No shit." He turned to look at the mass of bodies jumping up and down. "Thanks, man." And he was off.

Jump! Jump! Jump!

Jesse wiped his hands on a bar rag and evaluated the turn the evening had taken. Clarissa had crossed a major threshold in her recovery, and he'd just met a woman he found to be, to say the least, very interesting. He could see himself dating Eileen, dinner, dancing, a movie, maybe, and maybe more, a house with a white picket fence, a dog, two and a half kids...

Yet, in the back of his mind, a persistent nag ate at him, Deirdre, the saddest thing he'd ever seen, a true victim of the violence in this world.

People grieved in different ways, but her father had taken his grief to the extremes of revenge. Now he'd spend the rest of his life in prison, mostly thanks to the flash drive Jesse had given Detective Doherty with the indisputable video evidence of Kellerman's guilt. As just as that punishment was, it left Deirdre with no one to visit her, not that she'd ever notice, but he would know, and that bothered him to no end...

"I'm back." Eileen slinked onto the barstool, breaking into his thoughts of visiting Deirdre on a regular basis. "Clarissa's making time with Tommy. So, what's your story, Jess?"

He leaned in close enough to enjoy the sweet scent of her raven hair. "I almost robbed a bank once."

Jump! Jump! Jump!

Jim Keane

Born in the Bronx, **Jim Keane** holds a Bachelor of Arts in English from Mount Saint Mary College and has completed many creative writing courses. He's written several short stories and three novels and has more tomes in the works. Jim resides in Westchester, New York, with his family.

Jim Keane

Read More from Jim Keane

Astra's Revenge – a short story

When a syndicate assassin kills the mother of a circus fortune teller, he can run but he can't hide from Astra's black magic and her crystal ball.

The Midnight Train Murders – a novella

A disgraced journalist, hoping to regain his prestige, investigates the murder of passengers on the midnight train to Crotonville, a reporter's dream story that turns into a nightmare.

Gateway – a novel

A tragic encounter with a bullet-riddled man in a dark alley catapults computer-nerd Sean Calhoun into a deadly cat and mouse race to protect a stolen cell phone that can connect to the dead.

After Sunset – a novella

Kevin Tippler's wife has left him and taken their eight-year-old son with her, but to convince her to come back, he'll have to join AA, toss out all his booze, and survive an apocalyptic virus that turns its victims into raging mutants.

https://www.twbpress.com/authorjimkeane.html

Enjoy more short stories and novels by
many talented authors at

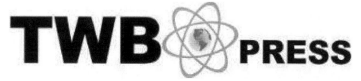

www.twbpress.com

Science Fiction, Supernatural, Horror, Thrillers,
Romance, and more

Made in the USA
Middletown, DE
29 August 2024

59755824R00152